John Binias's first novel was published by Macmillan in
February 2000. He works in television. In 1997, together
with Robbie Coltrane, he wrote a non-fiction book. He
has a degree in Philosophy, and a degree in Law, lives in
north London, and enjoys rock and ice climbing.

'Baffling, fiendishly odd, and amorally philosophical'
Big Issue

'Dark, but brilliantly funny . . . A clever and amusing
satire on the nature of love and the distractions of lust'
Yorkshire Post

Also by John Binias

Theory of Flesh

JOHN BINIAS

(ADVICE FOR TRAVELLERS)

PAN BOOKS

First published 2001 by Macmillan

This edition published 2002 by Pan Books
an imprint of Pan Macmillan Ltd
Pan Macmillan, 20 New Wharf Road, London N1 9RR
Basingstoke and Oxford
Associated companies throughout the world
www.panmacmillan.com

ISBN 0 330 48694 2

Copyright © John Binias 2001

The right of John Binias to be identified as the
author of this work has been asserted by him in accordance
with the Copyright, Designs and Patents Act 1988.

All rights reserved. No part of this publication may be
reproduced, stored in or introduced into a retrieval system, or
transmitted, in any form, or by any means (electronic, mechanical,
photocopying, recording or otherwise) without the prior written
permission of the publisher. Any person who does any unauthorized
act in relation to this publication may be liable to criminal
prosecution and civil claims for damages.

9 8 7 6 5 4 3 2 1

A CIP catalogue record for this book is available from
the British Library.

Typeset by SetSystems Ltd, Saffron Walden Essex
Printed and bound in Great Britain by
Mackays of Chatham plc, Chatham, Kent

This book is sold subject to the condition that it shall not,
by way of trade or otherwise, be lent, re-sold, hired out,
or otherwise circulated without the publisher's prior consent
in any form of binding or cover other than that in which
it is published and without a similar condition including this
condition being imposed on the subsequent purchaser.

To my parents

For much needed encouragement and advice, special thanks to Tanya Crawford, Paul Clark, Mic Cheetham, Peter Lavery, Alice Miles, Lucy Bolton, James Kean, Julie Swales, Joyce Binias, Derek Binias, Sarah Blenkinsop, Colm Long, Suzy Wilson, Rupert Girdham, and Martin Membery.

Life is a bridge: pass over it, but do not build a home upon it
Ancient Persian saying

contents

Contents

Loco /'leukeu/ $n.^1$ *colloq.* (abbrev. of LOCOMOTIVE) Of or pertaining to movement from one place to another; an engine which accomplishes this. **Loco** /'leukeu/ $n.^2$ *(US hist)* (abbrev. of LOCOFOCO) A radical, equal rights Democrat. **Loco** /'leukeu/ *adv.* (fr It *al loco*, at the place) To be played as written, not an octave higher. **Loco** /'leukeu/ $n.^3$ & a. **A** *n.* *(US slang)* Loco weed, marijuana. **B** *a.* mad, Insane, off your head.

(acknowledgements)

It used to annoy me that, whenever I let slip in conversation that both my parents died in a plane crash when I was a boy, the great majority of people would leap thoughtlessly to the conclusion that this event must have had a uniquely negative impact on my life. Throw my much-loved younger sister into the conflagration, and even apparently intelligent, educated people would start bandying the word 'tragedy' about willy-nilly, without having the least regard for the economic realities of the situation.*

Like many young people of good family, I had a lot

---

* Tragedy is an outdated concept. Its decline can be traced back to the sixteenth century, when double-entry bookkeeping was first invented. The double entry system requires that each and every transaction should appear in a person's account books twice, once as a debit and once as a credit. It is here the sharp-eyed literary historian will discover the origins of black comedy.

of capital tied up in my parents. They owned a large London townhouse, together with second, third, and fourth 'homes' in sundry meteorologically desirable locations around the globe. My father had a substantial portfolio of investments, and both father and mother had the foresight to insure their lives for sums of money that a person of moderate needs (if such a one can be imagined) might consider to be bordering upon the obscene. I did not strike the deal myself, but fair is fair, and I was not complaining.

As it happens, I have in my CD collection a copy of the black-box recording of the accident in which my family died. For the most part it is the usual banal affair, the flight crew maintaining a semblance of rationality by indulging in futile technical chit-chat concerning the difficulty they are experiencing in keeping their jumbo airborne, whilst in the background a chorus of hysterical and despairing screams resounds. And if, when I discern the plaintive cries of my mother and sister amidst the uproar, my heart breaks for them yet again, when I hear my father bellowing at them to stop making a fuss, his strangulated tone expressing simultaneously both the malice of the murderer and the anguish of his victim, my despair is so commingled with relief that an emulsion of immiscibles is formed and, in equal scale weighing delight and dole, I go shopping.

For my father had a distinctively positive outlook on

life, and never could abide that type of person who makes a show of their vulnerability, and creates a spectacle of their pain. Not that he was an unemotional man. Oh, no. He had a profound love of profit, and cared passionately about what he regarded as the disastrous post-war decline in standards of driving. I never will forget the day, extraordinary in the annals of popular motoring, when I saw him spit in the face of an elderly lady who had accidentally backed her car into his new limousine, faintly marking its nearside front wing. Fortunately, no one was seriously injured, though it has to be said that my concept of parental authority did not emerge from the incident wholly unscathed.

But this is beside the point. Because a jet-propelled commercial passenger aeroplane is by far the safest way of getting from a to b on the waterlogged crust of this god-forsaken globe of ours and, statistically speaking, one is less likely to be undone two miles above the earth's surface than cosying it in one's own home. Which just goes to show, anything can happen. Even to me.

(two alternative itineraries)

Independent travel is not so much an occupation, or even a recreation, as a state of mind. The Embankment Underground to Dalston Kingsland via Oxford Circus and Highbury & Islington, if one's mindset is that of the genuine explorer, can be every bit as rewarding as, let us say, Pretoria to the Tsodila Hills via Bloemfontein and Bophuthatswana, crossing the border with Botswana at McCarthy's Rust, speeding over the salt lake in a cloud of brilliant white dust to Tshabong, slipping smoothly between the head-high sandbanks that define the distinctly unmetalled track to Mabuasehube, where you might pass the night under canvas, disturbed only by the occasional lion's roar, before driving on to the great cattle town of Tshane, where you replenish your supplies of fresh water and biltong before passing back on to the tarmac. A right-hand turn at Ghanzi, followed four hours later by a left at Sehithwa (on the banks of the dry lake Wgami, where forest fire perchance threatens to engulf you) brings you out in Tau, where, exhausted, you check into a broken-down guesthouse, curl up under a mosquito net, and fall asleep, dreaming of darkness. The next day, at dawn, you hit the road once more, the light as clear as your mind is turbid with the plethora of new sensations you have experienced. Deftly locating the well-secreted left-hand turn that leads to the Tsodilo Hills, you pack the back of your Land Rover and perhaps the roof-rack too with *San* people, before grinding on through the bush for half a day or more, until the sacred hills finally reveal themselves to you in all their uncanny majesty, and you take refuge from the fury of the sun in the cool, naturally ventilated cave you discover – the jewel of your journey – nestling in the loins of the great Mother Hill.

The budget traveller may wish to choose a Toyota rather than a Land Rover, and may also prefer to avoid the overnight stop at Mabuasehube, where park fees are expensive; likewise, on the journey to Dalston Kingsland from the Embankment, they may wish to consider purchasing a travelcard, if further journeys by public transport are planned for the same day.

(the travel bug bites)

My last great expedition – the journey which will be the practical focus of this little manual – began among the brushed-steel fixtures and frosted-glass fittings of a fashionable London bar, where I was enjoying a quiet drink with my old acquaintance and tormentor, Max Mann. Max is an intellectual, a radical of sorts, who disagrees with everything I say and disapproves of everything I do. This much, at least, is clear. Why I tolerate his company at all is less easy to divine. Perhaps I do not care whether people hate me or not, just so long as they make their feelings clear well in advance of showing them. Yes, maybe it is not so much the blows I cannot bear as the shocks. And so I keep Max ready to hand, to keep me informed of what my conscience might say to me next time she gets in touch.

Conscience is a fickle friend, her moods unpredictable as forest fire and her intentions no less benevolent. She disappears for months on end without a word as to her whereabouts, only to appear on your doorstep unannounced, in the wee small hours of some sweet, dream-drenched night, smiling innocently, while a host of rowdy, drunken recriminations stand sniggering and sneering behind her back, looking for somewhere to party. With Max, on the other hand, I can decide for myself whether I wish to be hectored and harangued. I can choose the place where the inquisition will be held, and I can terminate the process of chastisement at will.

On this occasion, appropriately enough, I had just been extolling to Max the benefits of independent travel – which broadens the mind, stimulates the senses, discourages jingoism, challenges our conception of what it is to be human, reminds us that we are alive, teaches respect for otherness, encourages resourcefulness, keeps boredom at bay, and gets us out of the house. As examples of independent travellers who have made invaluable contributions to this rich tradition I cited Odysseus, Scott of the Antarctic, and Jesus Christ when he was on tour.

Max gave a snort and retorted by telling me that, in attempting to ameliorate the loneliness and emptiness of my life by travelling at great expense to far-flung corners of the globe, I was causing fragile ecosystems to be destroyed, age-old traditions to be prostituted, economically impoverished peoples to be corrupted, cultural

differences to be trivialized, and delicate social forma-
tions to be stressed beyond breaking point. Oh, and I
was squandering the world's precious supplies of fossil
fuels, and accelerating global warming en route. *Touché*,
Max!

I was about to point out to my dour interlocutor
that, were he able to afford something a little more
stimulating than the formulaic, pre-packaged experiences offered by the mass-market tour operators, he
might be tempted to acknowledge that there are two
sides to the coin. But, before I had so much as drawn
breath, he was explaining to me that the term 'independent traveller' was anyway an oxymoron.

According to Max, a traveller could only truly be
called independent if he or she walked everywhere, or
perhaps rode on horseback (having first reduced their
equine friend into captivity from the feral condition, or
having bred it from steeds they had domesticated earlier). During his or her journey this hypothetical traveller
would eat only victuals they had gathered, grown, trapped, netted, hooked, shot, butchered, prepared and
cooked themselves, using weapons and utensils of their
own devising.

When I asked whether a bicycle and home-made
sandwiches might not constitute a fair compromise, Max
grew vehement, pointing out that few if any individuals
in the world today possess the skills necessary to create

from scratch such a complex piece of machinery as a bicycle – which requires that iron be extracted from its ore, purified, thcn combined with carbon to make steel; that this steel be extruded into tubes; that those tubes be welded together to form a frame; that rubber is vulcanized and moulded to make tyres; and that chromium is mined and purified to coat the bell – a process that cannot be performed without a ready supply of electricity. And this is to say nothing of all the tools that would have to be manufactured before any of these processes could begin . . . etcetera, etcetera, etcetera.

'All right, all right,' I groaned, 'point taken. In future I'll walk everywhere. Satisfied?'

He was not. My concession had come too late to save me. 'As for the sandwiches,' he droned on, 'if you were to grow and grind the wheat yourself, using seedcorn gathered from the wild . . .'

'OK, I'll eat acorns,' I offered, desperate to shut him up.

'. . . and if you were to cultivate the yeast yourself,' he continued, 'and were to collect the water you needed from a spring; and if you were to bake the bread yourself in some kind of heat-proof container you yourself had manufactured, in some kind of elementary oven you had constructed yourself, using fuel you had gathered yourself, lit by a spark you generated yourself from a naturally occurring substance such as flint, which you yourself had sourced; and if you were to fill your sandwich with wild salad vegetables gathered from uncultivated heath or woodland; and if you were to carry these sandwiches in a pouch of leather, flayed and cured and sewn with your own hands, using a needle manufactured by yourself from some natural material, such as bone; then you would only be dependent upon other people for the road you were cycling on and the myriad technologies you employed in performing all this work – technologies which were developed over the course of millennia, and are the end product of the hard work and creativity of millions of people.'

Amen, Max. And your point is *what* exactly?

He paused. I was looking away, pretending not to listen. It wasn't difficult; I found his speech excruciatingly dull. But, what was more, my eye had been intrigued by an auburn-haired young woman who was standing at the other end of the bar with a small group of friends. So fascinated had I become by this woman's appearance, her gestures and expressions that, even after Max had ceased his tirade, I felt no inclination whatever to look back at him.

She was physically attractive – beautiful, even – but that was not all. There was something about her that was troubling me, something that I could not define. It had upon me the effect – and I speak roughly now – of pale yellow sunlight bursting through banks of gray cumulus cloud, cloud which had seemed never-ending, on a drear day in some steep-sided Norwegian fjord; a light which translates the dull gray of the granite cliffs into a blushing platinum, the unspoken darkness of the foliage into a joyful chorus of greens; a light which echoes from the playful surface of the sea in pearlescent cadenzas of aquamarine and ... other blues, blues too true to mention, blues without name, blues without number – blues that are, how can I put it, *commercially unavailable*. Yes, it was as when, while out strolling in a dense forest which one imagines to be flat – forest without limit, forest without respite – a wide open plain ringed by lofty mountain spires suddenly declares itself between two leaf-laden boughs. And perhaps, yes, perhaps it was just a little reminiscent of the effect a child's laughter might have upon the sullen, desolate beauty of the interior of a great Gothic cathedral, that reaches up to God as I* ... as I† ... reach down to tie my own shoelace.‡

'And if, after doing all this work,' Max added wittily, 'you felt remotely like going for a totally pointless and unproductive bicycle ride, you are without doubt an unusually energetic man.'

---

* I am struggling to express myself here.
† Once more into the fray.
‡ Got it!

Yes, Max. Very good, Max. And your point?

He paused, waiting for me to respond. I did not do so.

'So that's what I think of your so-called independent travel: it is an instance of dependency in its purest form,' he declared, attempting to goad me into acknowledging his existence. Finally, when it had become obvious to Max that I had found his speech so irrelevant I had failed even to notice that he had finished speaking, he turned around to see what I was gazing at.

'Hey, that's one of my students you're ogling,' he said.

As if from a great distance, Max's voice penetrated my reverie. I turned to him. 'Do you know her?' I asked.

He nodded. 'She's very bright.'

At this point, one of the woman's friends alerted her to the fact that she was being talked about. I indicated to Max that she was looking our way. Max turned to look back at her, and she smiled and waved. Whispering to her friends that she had seen a ditchwater lecturer from the university, whom prudence obliged her to acknowledge – together with a beguiling stranger, whose presence might just make the performance of this burdensome duty worthwhile, or even pleasant – she wandered over to greet us.

She walked slowly, displaying with every sinuous step the sort of confidence that cannot be simulated – the confidence that comes from finding one's gait early in life and sticking to it.

'Hello, Aphro,' said Max.

'Hello, Max,' replied Aphro.

Max turned to me. 'Aphro is one of my best students.'

Aphro blushed.

Realizing that he had embarrassed her, Max then attempted to make amends to her by humiliating me. 'This is Otto. Otto is a moneyed man of leisure – a *rentier* in the grand nineteenth-century style. He represents everything people like you and I detest. He's never done a day's work in his life, relies wholly on the labour of others, and yet resolutely insists that he's an *independent man* ... Otto and I get together for a drink now and then to knock lumps off each other, and find out what the enemy's thinking. It keeps us both in trim.' With this Max patted me on the shoulder, causing me to spill my beer down the front of my shirt.

Aphro laughed. She wasn't laughing at me, though. In fact, I'd go as far as to say she found me an intensely sympathetic and yet at the same time dignified figure. No, she was laughing because Max had made a joke; Max was her tutor, and she was obliged to keep on the right side of him. All the same, I was disappointed by her sycophantic attitude. Although I had not known her long, I had expected a loftier spirit.

Max and Aphro exchanged a few snippets of gossip

about the department where Max taught and Aphro studied, which unfortunately I could not decipher due to the sound of blood coursing through my head. Then Aphro returned to her friends. Perhaps because of the abruptness of her departure, which was every bit as unexpected as her arrival, or perhaps because I had not yet eaten anything that day, watching her go left me feeling cheated and abused.

Reflecting on the feelings she aroused in me, I quickly realized that there was something not quite normal about this girl, who was so easily amused as to appear almost simple-minded, who was almost pathetically eager to ingratiate herself with figures of authority, and who came and went without a word of explanation, crashing in and out of people's lives like some kind of crazy Greek deity. Yes, there was definitely something not quite normal about her.

Pondering thus, and finding it increasingly difficult to focus my attention on the pathetic jousts which Max continued to direct at my exceptionally high degree of personal freedom – which he resents as domestic cattle resent the deer that prance through their fields and bound so lightly over imprisoning fences – I listened to the swaying sound of the sea pulsating in my ears while nodding and smiling at Max with such apparent complaisance that he eventually ceased trying to rile me altogether and, peering awkwardly at me, asked me if I was feeling all right. I told him that, so far as I could tell, I was very well indeed. Then he asked me if there was anything on my mind. I shrugged and looked away.

Seeing that my head was turned once again in her general direction, Max leaped to the conclusion that I was gazing at Aphro. 'You could do worse than pushing some of your money in her direction, you know,' he said in that coarse, stolid way he has of reducing everything to the lowest common denominator.

I didn't understand what he meant, and was annoyed he should presume in his materialistic fashion that, simply because my eyes were pointing towards Aphro at the same time as being, as it were, 'focused' upon her face, my thoughts must be occupied with her too.

'She's a brilliant student, but she has to spend half her week doing shitty jobs in shops and offices and restaurants just to keep her head above water,' Max explained.

I shrugged. What did it have to do with me if someone's parents had failed to make adequate provision for their education? Hard work never hurt anyone, as my father used to say of his employees.*

'How's your golf game?' I asked, in a forthright, manly kind of way.

---

* It certainly never did me any harm.

Max looked puzzled. 'I don't play golf, Otto.'

'So?' I asked, nonchalantly. 'Why not start?'

'I've *never* played golf,' he insisted anxiously.

'I believe you,' I reassured him. 'Calm down, it's not your fault. I promise not to mention it again.'

'What's got into you tonight?' he asked.

At this point, for the simple reason that my eyes* still happened to be pointing towards that part of the bar, I noticed that Aphro was leaving. Her friends were remaining behind, but Aphro was departing. Presumably this was either because she could not afford to buy another drink, or because she had to be up early in order to do some studying before traipsing off to a humiliating and debasing day's labour in some slop shop, serving infected offal to *hoi polloi*. Whatever the explanation, the next thing I knew, she was gone.

Suddenly, I understood the full significance of what Max had been telling me. It was a disgrace that a young woman of parts should have her spiritual, aesthetic and intellectual development stifled by undeserved impecuniosity. Without a word, I went haring out of the bar and into the street.

---

* They are located on the front of my face, approximately four inches from my chin, one on either side of my nose. Henceforth, let no man accuse me of shirking my duty as a writer to describe the world as I see it.

I caught up with her at a junction fifty yards down the road, just as she was about to cross the road.

'Aphro,' I gasped.

She turned.

Looking at the ground, trembling slightly, I found myself wondering why I was feeling the cold so intensely, and whether I would have been better off with an overcoat of pure cashmere rather than the cashmere and wool mix I had chosen. A cashmere and wool mix is arguably less warm and certainly less luxurious to the touch, but it does boast greater longevity. But longevity is a quality in which, historically speaking, I have no interest, since I could quite easily afford to buy a new overcoat every day of the year, summer and winter alike, until the end of my natural life, if I so desired. Even so, there I was, standing in the street, clutching my coat to my sides, shivering like a urine-soaked oenophile.

'Hello, Otto,' she said, with startling simplicity.

'Hello, Aphro,' I replied, mimicking her words so closely I almost slipped into the obvious mistake of calling her 'Otto', which of course is my name.

At this point, Aphro unleashed a silence that went through me like a knife, or encompassed me like a net, or cradled me like a*

---

* My mind's a blank. Sorry.

'I've been thinking,' I declared, looking up at the sky, which was an extraordinarily pale shade of blue for the latitude. It was that kind of faded, translucent, whitish blue that one sees in the summer skies of northernmost Scandinavia, and which seemed to me in those days somehow to symbolize the leeching away of all emotion from the world, and which was also, for reasons that lie beyond the scope of the present book, my favourite colour.

'Yes?' said Aphro, smiling at me warmly, as if thinking was an activity she always liked to encourage.

'Max happened to mention to me that you sometimes found it necessary to work.'

Aphro looked surprised, and then laughed. Apparently I had made a joke.

'I mean, to work for money.'

Aphro nodded, though the effect of my witticism lingered on in the corners of her eyes, which were brown, and possessed the same wave-particle duality that is traditionally ascribed to photons of light. As particles they were moist, wide, warm, and forgiving, while as waves they lapped at my soul like musical water.

She was looking expectantly at me, with an air of generosity that made me feel that, however determined I might be to get things wrong, she really did want me to get them right. Encouraged, I continued. 'The thing is, it just so happens that I myself have . . . I myself have been considering employing someone. I've been considering it for some time . . .'

Aphro smiled politely. Obviously, more was required. I racked my brains for the right story. I didn't have a garden, I didn't run a business, and I didn't have any correspondence that couldn't be handled in five minutes with a cheque book and a shredder. It could only be one thing. I gritted my teeth. Her hair was very glossy; parcels of electromagnetic radiation from the visible spectrum bounded to and fro it like children at a fun fair. 'I need someone to live in my house and . . . and do things.'

Aphro raised her eyebrows. Whether this was because she was sincerely interested in the offer I was making I could not tell.

'What things?' she asked bluntly.

'Homely things,' I said, with an ambiguity that surprised even me, practised though I was in the art of circumlocution.

Aphro stared at me hard. She must have understood perfectly, because the very next thing she said to me was, 'You're not making sense, Otto.'

A fine way for a prospective employee to talk to her prospective employer!

'*Domestic* things,' I said, in a tone that suggested her pedantry was forcing me to make absurdly fine discriminations of meaning.

'You mean, you want me to be your maid?' asked Aphro. I really couldn't tell if she was offended or not, her manner was so matter-of-fact. She spoke to me as if she were helping a very young child to express itself.

'Well . . .' I hesitated, '. . . yes and no. I mean, *maid* is such an old-fashioned term, is it not? And ambiguous too, in its way . . .'

Aphro's eyes narrowed as she waited for me to explain myself. I declined to do so.

'So what *are* you saying, Otto?' she insisted, her manner suddenly rather brusque. She shifted her weight on her feet, as though preparing for flight.

'I'm saying, like a maid in that you might like to do a bit of housework now and then, and perhaps cook once in a while – though to be honest, I'm not a great one for eating at home, and I've never been bothered by a bit of dust. And then again, unlike a maid in that . . . in that *maid*, derived as it is from the term *maiden*, could be taken to imply both that you are a young woman, for instance – which of course you are – but also other things – things that pertain intimately to your womanhood, but would be of no significance whatsoever within our professional relationship.'

I juddered to a halt. What was I saying? I repeated my words over to myself. Even I could not easily construe them. I felt like someone who, plunging down a

cliff, squanders his last seconds in analysing the prepos-
terous nature of his stumble.

I flattered myself that the look Aphro was giving me
was rueful. But it could just as easily have been bristling
with contempt. She was, after all, an intelligent woman. I
couldn't tell, because I couldn't see a damned thing.
Brightly coloured pennants were fluttering invisibly before
my eyes, signifying the imminent arrival of an implacable
enemy, come to destroy me. Technically speaking, it was
her turn to speak. But when one party in a colloquy talks
gibberish, convention dictates that the rule of turn and
turn about is suspended, until adequate reparations have
been made.

'Not to worry,' I said. 'I'm not there half the time
anyway, and I've always taken pride in looking after
myself. I'm quite an independent soul, really.' I paused.
Aphro was staring at me as though I were a heavily
vegetated inscription. 'I certainly don't need mothering,
if that's what you're thinking,' I said, with a desperately
off-hand laugh.

Aphro flinched. She actually looked rather upset. I
felt confused. I couldn't see how I could have offended
her *that* much.

'I see I've offended you. It doesn't matter. I only
asked because you could have set your own salary –
within reason, of course. We could have linked it to one

of the senior grades in the civil service, for instance. You could have started off at assistant undersecretary level. And you could have lived with me – I mean in my flat – which is quite large enough for two. And you could have lived there rent-free, you see, because I was talking to Max about your academic career, and I really respect the work you're doing, and I wanted to help.

'Anyway, I guess I'll see you around when I get back from my next trip abroad, which will probably be an extremely long one. I expect Max told you that I travel a lot. And by then you will have finished your degree and moved away from London. So I don't suppose we'll be seeing much of each other any more.' I hesitated. Aphro was looking at me with renewed interest, as if, having satisfied herself that I was a maniac, she still couldn't quite decide whether I was a benevolent or a malicious one.

'Why?' she asked. She appeared to be settling down a little. That is to say, she remained in an upright position, balanced precariously on two feet – as is the way with adult *Homo sapiens* – but no longer appeared to be preparing to make a dash for safety.

'Why what?' I replied, innocently.

'Why are you offering me this . . . job?'

'I just told you. You look like you need the money,' I replied.

'Well, thanks,' she replied, justifiably offended.

Another silence followed. Silences, in my view, are there to be filled, by force if necessary. 'I was attempting to promote learning,' I said, somewhat feebly, but not without a hint of tetchy pride. My remark had no effect on the baffled, almost sullen look on my unfortunate interlocutor's face. I turned to go.

'Wait,' Aphro said.

I turned. The sky had changed colour, from pale blue to light black. Aphro was taking a pen from her bag. She tore a scrap of paper out of her diary, scribbled something on it, and offered it to me.

'I have to go now. If you really want me to ... to come and work for you, give me a ring tomorrow, or whenever. Ring me when you're sober and we'll discuss it.'

I stared at the scrap, which appeared to be made out of perfectly ordinary white paper. Then I took it from her. It was very small but, even so, our fingers did not touch as it passed from hers to mine. That said, in the two hundred million or so nanoseconds it took for me to grasp and for her to release the fragment, one or two molecules of oxygen, or what is more likely atoms of nitrogen, may possibly have had time to follow a violently erratic zigzag course, from her skin to mine, from my skin to hers, so proximate were our extremities. So, in a sense, we touched.

I raised the paper to my face. Incredibly, it had on it a series of digits, together with the word 'Aphro', spelt as I have spelt it here. I'm no mathematician, but the series of numerals looked anything but arbitrary, and I felt convinced it must be a telephone number. For some obscure reason – possibly to do with a childish association with the pyramids of Egypt, which I have always loved for their bold eschewal of commercial values – this triangular scrap of paper pleased me immensely.

I succeeded in aborting what, if nature had been allowed to run its course, could easily have grown into a full-blown smile (though the embryo was so slightly formed when its development was terminated that it might equally well have been a scream, a snigger, or even a sneeze), before declaring to Aphro – with great nobility of spirit, almost as if it was she who had insulted me – 'I'm leaving town very soon.'

'Well, whatever,' Aphro replied, with a perplexed, embarrassed shrug, obviously pained by what could only appear to her – as to myself, and no doubt to you too – to be the rapid, incoherent mood swings of a lunatic.

'I'll ring first thing,' I declared, eager as a schoolboy.

She smiled – a response which, in the face of behaviour as strange as mine, showed a good deal of courage and great resilience of humour. Here is a woman of character, I said to myself.

We said goodnight and Aphro left me. I walked back

to the bar, keeping strictly to the kerb, taking good care to touch neither the pavement nor the road. Somehow I even managed to shimmy around a postbox that protruded directly into my path; passers-by were delighted by my display of acrobatic virtuosity, for which I demanded no payment.

Though I moved swiftly as the wind, by the time I reached the bar Max had left.

(getting trippy)

It takes more than one kind of trip to make a holiday, and one man's analgesic is another man's route to spiritual enlightenment – which brings me to the vexed subject of recreational drug use. Now, as we all know, the 'abuse' of mood-altering drugs – other than those sanctioned by custom – is often regarded as an ethically dubious practice. But it must be remarked that the grounds advanced in support of this judgement are at best thin and at worst inconsistent.

Foremost among the arguments levelled against the non-medicinal use of narcotics is that they offer a 'quick fix' or an 'easy way out' – that is to say, they provide a source of immediate pleasure and release that threatens to undermine an individual's or even a whole society's character. That one seldom hears the same argument levelled against teabags or flushing lavatories is hardly worth remarking upon. Far more important is the strong body of empirical evidence that exists to show that, in the case of drugs – as opposed to teabags and modern plumbing – the accusation is simply untrue.

Indeed, it is untrue even according to the rhetoric of the anti-drugs campaigners. For do they themselves not take pains to alert us to the emaciated, demoralized, disease-ridden condition of the waifs who have become addicted to this or that substance, precisely in order to make the opposite point? Drugs are a quick and easy route to nothing more satisfying than nausea, vomiting, physical torment, disease, and failure.

No, if you hope to extract any real benefit from the increasingly wide and sophisticated range of narcotics that are ever more readily available to consumers in the UK, you must be prepared to put your back into it. Energy and determination are all. I have tried all types of regimen, ranging from total abstinence – usually coupled with two or three excellent meals a day, a brisk, invigorating walk through rousing countryside, together with a modicum of skiing, mountaineering, sub-aqua diving, parascending, bungee jumping, white-water rafting, etcetera – to the other 'extreme' of weeks or even months spent in a self-induced narcotic haze, with all the inspirational highs and despondent lows, the crazed insanitary dreams, the camaraderie, the solitude, and the twitching paranoia that such a lifestyle entails.

I flatter myself that this experience puts me in an

ideal position to judge which lifestyle is the hardest 'work', and which places the greatest demands upon an individual's character, if personal annihilation is to be avoided. And I feel bound to say, in my experience, it is the latter. Drug abuse is not, as the campaigners often portray it, something one can simply slip into by accident. Indeed, in my view it is not so much a recreation as a vocation – even, in some cases, a full-blown calling. Certainly, it is not for the faint-hearted.

But, in common with all exacting and difficult tasks (such as warfare, playing a musical instrument to a high standard, and the more extreme paraphilias), along with its self-imposed stringencies, self-intoxication brings its own special rewards; rewards which I for one would hate to be without for more than two or three weeks at a time. Not least amongst these benefits is the occasional well-earned hallucination in which it seems that God is a coherent concept, the rich are happier than the poor, and all is well with the world. Indeed, I have sometimes had delusional perceptions of this type that have lasted, quite literally, for seconds on end.

If the politicians ever discover a genuine moral argument against recreational drug use, presumably they will share it with us. But perhaps not: politicians are unpredictable creatures, as anyone is bound to be who spends their time attempting to second-guess the preferences of rational human beings, about whose lives they understand nothing.* But whether they tell us or not, we'll be sure to find out if the politicians do discover such an argument, because they're not *complete* idiots, and if they ever happened across a genuinely convincing case against narcotics, they and their loved ones would almost certainly stop using them. I've asked my supplier to keep me in touch with how his sales are going upriver; if I hear anything untoward I'll let you know.

Turning at last to the practical issues regarding drug abuse, such as what to take and how often to take it, I'd like to introduce you to a system I have developed, which I call *circuit abuse*. I took the idea from my personal trainer, who recommends an analogous system to help impede the body's natural propensity to decay. The main advantage of circuit abuse is that it reduces the chances of becoming dependent on any one substance, while at the same time decreasing the impact that any one particular chemical might have on one's long-term health. Uppers can be alternated with downers, precipitators of psychosis with drugs that inflict disorder

---

*   Have you ever watched a shoal of fish flickering coinstantaneously this way and that, in response to who knows what subliminal stimuli? The fish at the front that can't quite keep up with the others – the fish that has to glance behind in order to find out what the other fish are doing before it decides which way to turn – that fish is their *political leader*.

upon the personality, in such a way as to avoid potentially embarrassing extremes of behaviour.

Like its somewhat less demanding cousin, circuit training, circuit abuse requires iron discipline, together with a willingness to experiment with the composition and duration of the circuit. Some people like to include periods of total sobriety ('lying fallow'), while others prefer to keep stumbling round and round in circles ('rotating') until exhaustion finally fells them. In practice, everyone must find a routine to suit themselves, so I will not delve into questions of detail. But I would recommend that you keep to a well-balanced diet, taking care to eat plenty of fresh fruit and vegetables, and that you combine your routine of circuit abuse – however challenging it may seem in its own right – with regular physical and mental exercise.

Failure to observe these three golden rules can quickly lead to intellectual and physical atrophy. Take care that your regular doses of your favourite chemicals do not gradually creep upwards, with no appreciable change in the degree of stimulation, sedation, or whatever it is that the drug produces. When you no longer enjoy your drug abuse, but find it necessary to continue none the less, alarm bells should be sounding – although, realistically, by this stage you will in all likelihood be unable to differentiate a good day from a bad one. And neither will you care.

Jabbering nonsense in an empty room; inexplicable
bouts of muteness; failure to move from your sofa
(*chaise longue*, garden shed, Bath chair, Persian rug,
kitchen floor) for days at a time; solitary screaming fits;
uncontrollable bouts of sobbing; scrofulous, corpselike
eruptions on the skin: all these can be useful warning
signs. But do remember that the significance of such
symptoms can vary considerably, depending on family
and educational background.

None the less, I firmly believe that, if you have plenty
of free time, together with an iron will and a reasonable
degree of financial security, there's no reason why care-
ful application of the 'circuit abuse' method should not
result in a significant reduction in general levels of pain,
boredom, despondency, flashbacks, self-contempt, anxiety, exasperation, despair, futility, confusion, and nihil-
ism which, combined in the right quantities, constitute
the well-ordered soul.

(a journey downmarket)

Love is the last remaining human good that remains
fairly and squarely outside the domain of the money
economy.* The evident resistance of this particular service to the process of commodification, and the conse-
quent continuance of what, to all intents and purposes,
amounts to a pre-modern economy based upon the principle of direct exchange, is of particular interest to the
independent traveller, who may find themselves far away
from home, in a foreign city, thousands of miles from
family and friends, in desperate need of a girlfriend or
boyfriend who loves them.†

This is a need that may overtake a healthy person at
almost any time of the day or night (though seldom, in

---

*   Lennon and McCartney, 1964.
†   What Max would term a 'partner' – as if fucking someone was of no
     more spiritual significance than playing bridge with them!

my experience, during mealtimes). It is entirely normal, and is best understood as a natural consequence of the hours, days, weeks, months, or even years of lonely self-reliance that the truly independent traveller subjects themselves to, in search of their promised land.

In my view, the best way of coping with the distress and unhappiness that failure to satisfy this need may cause is to pay a visit to one of the many loving girl-friends and boyfriends, in cities, towns, and hamlets around the globe, who are willing to make a direct exchange, love for love, at very short notice.

A word of warning: although such relationships are essentially based upon the principle of unmediated bar-ter, some kind of contribution towards the girlfriend's or boyfriend's rent and housekeeping is generally expected. This is often little more than a token sum, and is best regarded as a gratuity – an acknowledgement that, although these love-traders are in no way venal, nevertheless we live in a mercenary world, and love is no more capable of paying the rent than it is of affecting US treasury-bond yields. And, if I may for a moment assume what is for me at least an uncharacteristically dry and unemotional attitude, when one thinks about it this is no more than would be expected were one to share a flat or house with a girlfriend or boyfriend on a permanent basis.

So enamoured of this system of direct barter did I

become during one particularly long and emotionally arduous trip to south-east Asia that, upon returning to London, I decided to find for myself just such a 'short order' girlfriend who, in return for the love and affection I felt and showed towards her, would happily give me all the love and affection I needed in return, with only the briefest period of advance notice.

Sue and I were together for several years.* Because I was often away from home, and because when I was at home I did not always feel the need for the comfort and succour provided by a long-term relationship, which can be emotionally demanding in itself, we regularly spent long periods apart, during which we neither saw nor spoke to one another. This was not because we did not love each other dearly; rather it was because we were both fierily independent spirits, who guarded our liberties jealously, and preferred to cry ourselves to sleep in the comfort of our own respective bathrooms than inflict our sorrows upon each other, with all the risk of mutual dependency that course entails. In short, Sue had her life and I had mine; that is the way we liked it and that, I sincerely hoped, was the way it would remain.

She was a thoroughly modern woman, who never expressed the slightest interest in 'settling down' to breed. No, she was far too absorbed in her career for

---

* Sue is a lovely name, is it not? I chose it myself.

that. I forget exactly what it was she did but, whatever it was, it seemed to pay fairly well, because, although she was only nineteen (she had just turned sixteen when we first met – at least, I very much hope that she had) Sue had a very pleasant flat in a charming Georgian terraced house in the bustling heart of London's Soho.*

Some readers, no doubt, will imagine that an arrangement such as the one Sue and I shared can be little more sustaining or satisfying than a casual sexual encounter with a stranger, such as one might enjoy in a bar, a nightclub, an auction room, a garden party, a department store, an accident and emergency room, a hovercraft, an arboretum, or a zoo. In order to convince you that this is not so, I will give you a brief account of the last time Sue and I shared an evening of love. Our tryst took place no more than two or three days prior to that fateful night with Max, when I first conceived the idea of employing a domestic.

I had been to see a film.† When I was finally forced

---

* Although in the past Soho has (rightly, in my view) been perceived as a somewhat seedy area – hardly a proper place for a respectable career woman to make her home – in recent years the area has improved rapidly, as the civilizing influence of the large number of gay men who come there in the evenings in order to socialize has gradually made itself felt, and the previously overwhelming concentration of back-stabbing media types has been diluted.

† *L'Atalante*****, 1934, dir. Jean Vigo; a gripping account of a daring

by the usher to leave the uterine tranquillity of the cinema, the evening tide of commuters was ebbing at maximum velocity. Wandering north over Waterloo Bridge with no clear destination in mind, driven by some nomadic instinct away from my own flat, which is on the South Bank of the Thames, I found myself swept along in a whirling eddy of commuters. Unlike the greasy brown Thames – that rainy entrail of England, which slithers towards its North Sea resting place like so much grave slime – this human tide seemed to flow in all directions at once. Dour-suited businessmales and businessfemales were weaving in and out of one another's paths, each ravelling a thread which, knitted together, formed a single coarse fabric of homeward-bound humanity.*

And whither am I bound? I asked myself. To my empty flat? To the cinema again, to watch, again, someone else's hallucination of loneliness and death? To meet a friend in some trendy sterile bar, to drink, unthirstingly, glass after glass, while listening to them, to me, droning on about the difficulty involved in having it all,

---

voyage along the Seine by barge, set to a hauntingly beautiful ditty by Maurice Jaubert.

* Why they were not riding in taxis, God only knows. If one does not earn enough during the course of the day to enable one to travel home in some kind of elementary comfort, I cannot see the point of going to work in the first place.

keeping it, and then acquiring more? To a restaurant, to watch some waitress milk me sweetly for a tip? Or to Max's hovel, to be berated for my good fortune? Never, never, never, never, never. Then where?

It was at that moment I remembered Sue. I hadn't seen her for months. Suddenly, I felt desperately guilty for paying her so little attention. She would be lonely in her flat, perhaps even despairing. My mind was made up: There was no time to lose. I must go to her, and prove to her that she was not forgotten. I must go to her, to share with her the great longing I felt for her company, her solidarity, and her warmth (a longing which was so profoundly pent-up that until that moment it had altogether escaped my notice). I must go to her, to hold her in my arms and caress her, kissing her face and lips until she was finally roused from the wan, abandoned stupor in which she was no doubt languishing.

After a brief tussle with a commuter who was carrying a steel-reinforced briefcase and knew very well how to use it, I secured a cab.

'Greek Street,' I instructed the cabbie.

'You'd be better off walking at this time of day, mate,' he said to me, with winning frankness.

'I've got a bad leg,' I lied.

'Hop in, then,' he quipped. His attempt at humour offended me. If it wasn't for the fact that I was not in any way disabled I would have taken his number down and reported him to the Public Carriage Office. Putting my chagrin behind me, I took out my mobile phone. By the time we reached the Strand I had autodialled Sue's number.*

'Hello?'

The voice sounded vague – welcoming yet somehow wary; unfamiliar, even. I cursed myself for having allowed such a long period of time to elapse since last telling Sue that I loved her.

'Sue?' I said.

'Who is this?' said Sue curiously – sounding suspiciously as though she had forgotten not only the sound of my voice, but also her own name. No doubt she was depressed. Though her apparent mental vacancy could equally well have been a symptom of her somewhat excessive – indeed, nigh on habitual – experimentation with recreational narcotics. I made a mental note to query her about the state of her health.

'It's Otto.'

'Oh, Otto!' she replied, her diction suddenly vitalized by the joy of recognition.

'I'm coming round,' I said.

'When?' she asked, clearly anxious to see me as soon as possible.

'Now,' I declared. There was a pause. 'I'm in a cab,' I

---

* My publisher thought it wiser not to include the number here. Sorry.

continued. There was another pause. I looked out of the window. 'On Lower Regent Street,' I concluded.

'Hang on,' said Sue, somewhat sharply. No doubt excited by my sudden proximity, she appeared to have dropped the phone on a table, or perhaps on to the floor, for I heard an awful clatter. Then I heard footsteps, followed by muffled voices. It seemed the poor girl was talking to herself. More footsteps followed, then she picked the receiver up again. 'That's fine,' she said.

'Darling!' I cried.

'You can't stay long, mind.'

'I'm busy too,' I said. My words were met by silence. 'I'll be with you in a minute,' I reassured her, and rang off.

Less than ten minutes later I was pressing the bell for Sue's flat.

'Hello?' It was Susan's voice. My heart trilled.

'Susan, it's Otto.'

The buzzer sounded and the door clicked open. I mounted the stairs two at a time to find the door to Sue's flat standing ajar. Without knocking, I pushed the door open and stepped boldly across the threshold. Sue was in the bedroom, attending to her toilet.

'Susan,' I declared.

'Hang on, love,' she called out, so intent on her *maquillage* that she hardly turned to look at me.

'You don't have to do that for me,' I told her. 'Not after all these years.'

'Yeah,' she agreed, but continued working dutifully on her eyelashes even so. 'I'll be with you in a minute. Make yourself at home.'

I followed Sue's advice, perching awkwardly on the edge of the fluorescent green sofa and staring at the ceiling. The woodchip effect covering was fascinating. It had been cleverly painted to simulate the precise appearance of faded, unpainted, peeling woodchip paper, an effect of almost unbearable nostalgia. As I gazed upwards, several small patches of rogue colour – some brown, some a rusty red – attracted my attention. In my state of heightened romantic excitement, one of these patches appeared to have attached to it a clump of human hair. An optical illusion, no doubt; even so, I felt myself shudder as a wave of nausea gripped me. The extraordinary notions that one is subject to, when the amorous feelings are running high! That there should be blood, hair, and perhaps even human excrement smeared on the ceiling of Sue's flat – the very idea! I looked away in anguish.

A moment later Sue emerged from her boudoir. She recognized me immediately.

'Michael!' she declared. 'It's so nice to see you.'

'Sue,' I said to her, in all simplicity.

A brief silence followed, as we each took stock of the

myriad ways in which the other had changed – changes so subtle as to be invisible to all but a lover's omnivorous eyes. Sue was wearing a garnet-coloured leather skirt, fishnet stockings gules, and a polyester blouse with a wide Seventies-style collar in a lemon-yellow fabric upon which was printed a pattern showing what appeared to be pills and capsules of various colours, shapes and sizes. Having sated her eyes on my strangely familiar face, she glanced briefly at the clock on the mantelpiece, then looked back at me and smiled broadly. 'So what do you want to do, then?' she asked.

'What, this evening?' I asked, sounding surprised. Sue looked at me as though I was being very stupid and very annoying. 'I thought you said you were busy?' I continued, by way of explanation.

'I thought you said *you* were,' she said, smiling, but without being able to prevent the faintest hint of depression and resentment from inflecting her voice.

Another silence developed, this one a little less intimate than the last.

'How was your day?' I asked her.

'Fine,' she said, noncommittally. 'How was yours?'

'I'm very well, thank you,' I replied. 'Just back from Java . . . oh, two months ago, and I'm off to New York, oh, next week, or the week after that . . .'

'All right for some, innit?' said Sue, doing a hilariously

exact impression of a tart from the Isle of Dogs who sucks cocks round the back of King's Cross station to earn money to feed a heroin addiction. I laughed. Sue relaxed.

'So, what do you want to do, then?' she asked again, smiling cheekily.

'Come here and sit down with me,' I suggested, patting the sofa. 'Come and sit here so we can get to know each other again.'

She did so.

'We haven't seen each other for ages,' I said.

'No,' she agreed, somewhat guardedly. I sensed that she was hiding her true feelings.

'I . . . missed you,' I said somewhat hesitantly, glancing down at my pristine light tan suede brogues.

'Did you? That's funny,' said Sue, somewhat awkwardly. For a moment I wondered whether she mistakenly thought I had been addressing my shoes.

'Yes, I did,' I cooed cajolingly.

'That's nice,' said Sue.

We sat together, immersed in silence, sharing the moment. Sue glanced at the clock.

'You're a *naughty* boy, aren't you?' she asked me at last.

'I . . . I'm not sure,' I replied, feeling genuinely uncertain as to whether I fitted this description or not.

Perhaps she was referring to the fact that I had not called her for such a long time.

'Yes, you are,' she insisted in a childish voice. Then she leaned across to me and spoke directly in my ear. 'I remember what you did last time you came,' she whispered playfully.

As it happened, I myself could not remember. In order not to offend her, I played along. 'Can you, indeed?' I intoned, in no less a playful, no less sing-song a voice.

'Ye-es, I ca-an,' Sue sang back. The room, I noticed, was warm. Sue must have felt it too, for, casually undoing the top button of her blouse, she rearranged her collar in such a way that her fine white breasts – of which she is justifiably proud – might cool off a little. Without really looking, I gained the impression that she was wearing a red bra.

'That's a bit racy,' I said, sounding a little more shocked than I had intended.

'Do you think so?' she asked me, seeming genuinely interested. Peeking downwards, she tugged open the front of her blouse. The buttons slipped easily from their holes and the soft, warm flesh of Sue's breasts and belly were exposed. Her breasts were naturally very firm and, with the help of an underwired bra, seemed positively to be reaching out to greet me.

'Do you think it's *too* racy?' she asked somewhat

coyly, while at the same time displaying that perfect trust and composure that can only exist between people who have been sexual intimates for many years.*

'Not *too* racy, no,' I murmured. 'Just, you know, *racy*.'

'Good,' she said, giggling sensuously. 'I thought for a moment you were going to make me take it off.'

I considered her proposition. While I was thinking about it, Sue glanced nervously at the clock. Then, as she looked back towards me, she slipped off her stiletto-heeled slingbacks and subtly laid one of her legs across my lap, allowing her foot to brush suggestively against my loins as she did so. Sue has wonderfully straight, slim legs, with delicate ankles and fine, smooth knees that have always seemed to me to be purpose-built for worship.

'This is nice,' I said.

'Yeah,' she agreed.

'I mean, it's really nice to see you.'

'I couldn't agree more,' she said in a strangely mechanical tone.

I put my arm around her. Or rather, I attempted to put my arm around her, but Sue appeared to misread my intentions, because a moment later she had her head

---

* I almost said sexual *inmates* – how funny – for that is the last thing we were!

six inches from my lap and was tugging expertly at my fly.

'No!' I shouted. Sue jolted upright. She was shocked and, I think, a little hurt. I felt guilty; I had spoken too sternly to her. She had, after all, only been trying to express the very natural affection she felt for me.

'Wait,' I said, speaking more gently now, 'not yet.'

'Sorry,' she said meekly. Even so, I could see that I had offended her.

'Let's talk,' I suggested.

'All right,' she said, sitting up and rearranging her long, strawberry-blonde hair, which, strangely, seemed to have slipped slightly to one side, leaving her fringe lopsided.* 'What do you want to talk about?'

I thought for a few moments. 'About ... me and you,' I said at last, treating her to a little-boy grin, followed by a delicate little sigh, and at the same time experiencing the first, faint hint of an erection.

'What about me and you?' she snapped, feigning bafflement and frustration.

'Well,' I said, 'we've known each other for a long time now ...'

'Yeah,' she said, 'all right.'

---

* Unless it was her eyes that had slipped. But, all things being equal, scientific rationality compels me to accept the simplest and most elegant explanation: her scalp was only loosely attached to her head.

There was a moment's silence as we both reflected on the wonderful times we had had together. 'Do you remember that time when I was around here and the police knocked on the door?' I asked.

Sue appeared amazed by my powers of recall. 'Was that you?' she asked.

'Was that me?' I demanded, with dudgeon. 'Who else could it have been?'

'Yeah ... well then,' said Sue uncertainly, looking increasingly uncomfortable.

'You almost got into trouble that day,' I reminded her.

'I'm a naughty girl, Alan,' she said.

We sat in silence for a few more moments. Finally, I began to feel that our old intimacy had returned in full. I felt thoroughly *at home* with this woman. The clump of human hair that appeared somehow to have become attached to the woodchip ceiling no longer concerned me. I sighed again.

'This is nice,' I said once more, leaning back on the dizzying green sofa and stretching out my legs.

Sue was looking at me intently, her breasts and belly still exposed. 'What about a tit-wank?' she suggested sweetly, reaching out and resting one hand upon my knee. 'I do good tit-wanks. Everybody says so.'

Darling girl! Never a thought for herself!

I smiled. 'You're very sweet – do you know that, Sue?'

'You're sweet too – darling,' she replied, with a sudden moroseness in her manner that seemed so genuine that it could not fail to arouse me.

She brought me off in about fifteen seconds flat, which must count as something of a record even for me. I gave her a contribution towards her housekeeping – nothing really, hardly enough to pay for a decent dinner. As I left I attempted to kiss her on the cheek, a gesture which for some reason she felt the need forcibly to resist. Perhaps she was still smarting from my prolonged absence, and the kiss I was offering her seemed too much like yet another goodbye.

'You're a darling,' I told her, 'a real darling.'

'Yeah,' she murmured vaguely, slipping the money I had given her into a drawer. 'Come back soon, right?'

I gave her a lingering smile, then left swiftly, so as not to prolong the pain of parting.

As I was walking down the stairs, it struck me for the first time just how much I meant to this young woman, who lived in isolation from her family, whose friends were too busy to take anything but a passing interest in her well-being, and who devoted so much of her youthful time and energy to her career. This realization saddened me, but at the same time it brought solace. For it is a beautiful thing to be needed, is it not? I made a mental note to go back and see her soon.

Later, as I stood on the street corner, languidly waving

my hand for a cab, watching as the rush-hour retreat to the burbs segued into the evening influx of city-bound pleasure-seekers, my thoughts returned to my own life, and I found myself reflecting on my good fortune in having been born free from the chains of economic necessity, with no need to debase myself by selling my labour – as do barristers, for instance, and cabinet ministers, and carpet fitters. No, I would never have to work in order to provide myself with life's necessities – would never be obliged to fardels bear – for I was free.

Free!

(expedition support staff)

When selecting expedition support staff, who will be expected to provide essential back-up services during long journeys into uncharted interiors etcetera, a high degree of physical integrity can be crucial.

It may have been too soon to make such judgements, but I came away from my admittedly cursory, casual, and eminently disinterested first interview with Aphro with the distinct impression that her conformation was harmonious, her action graceful and fluid, her posture noble yet wholly devoid of arrogance, her figure shapely, her physiognomy symmetrical – exquisitely delicate and at the same time highly original – her hair as smooth and soft as a starling's plumage, her skin translucent, roseate and, so far as I could see, without flaws of any kind. In short, I detected no obvious physical defects.

This total absence of biogenetic glitches is a rare quality to find in a human being, but even so, it's worth keeping your eyes open for. More important still, however, where work of this kind is concerned, is an individual's character. Excellence of character is not much discussed these days. This is understandable, because, unlike physical beauty, it's devilishly difficult to turn a profit from. Indeed, economic science suggests that virtue is something of a dog where the balance sheet is concerned, and that the wealth of nations depends to a large degree upon the cultivation of three key vices in the population – dumb acquisitiveness in consumers, craven venality in employees, and never-ending rapaciousness in businessleaders and investors.

But, while I would never dream of challenging the instrumental value of such character traits for the economy at large, where expedition management is concerned other qualities come immediately to the fore. After all, when suspended from the wrist-loops of your ice-axes on the North Face of some near-vertical unclimbed peak in the Himalayas, nauseated and practically asphyxiated by the effect of altitude, your whole body trembling with exhaustion and fear, the last thing you want is the manager of your base camp contacting you on the radio, drunk on fermented yak's milk, demanding a pay rise. So it is that when choosing expedition support staff, such economically undesirable character traits such as loyalty, temperance, etcetera, come into their own.

This is why, during my first interview with Aphro, I

(rather furtively) behaved on purpose like a tongue-tied buffoon, in order to find out whether she would scoff at me, as an arrogant, irascible, intolerant person might. But she did not. Indeed, judging by her demeanour on that occasion, she seemed really to have that generosity of spirit that sets the merely obedient apart from the truly good. Certainly, Max spoke highly of her. All in all, although our meeting had been brief, I came away with a sneaking suspicion that Aphro was in all likelihood the most loyal, sensible, honest, brave, wise, fair-minded, friendly, generous, humorous, restrained, modest, patient, passionate, sensitive, loving person I had ever met. Lastly, if what Max had told me was anything to go by, her intellectual ability and originality were a delight to all who knew her.

Reflecting on these facts the day after our initial interview, I realized that my first impression of her had indeed been correct: Aphro was a complete oddball.

It can be difficult to know how to respond to such severe abnormality in a twenty-two-year-old woman. The uncanny sense of estrangement one feels when faced with someone who seems on the surface to be a perfectly ordinary human being yet who, the moment one scratches that surface, turns out to be utterly unique and exceptional, falling way outside normal distribution curves, can cause a kind of hysterical, panicky, ecstasy. As a seasoned traveller, however, who has seen his share of exceptional sights, I was peculiarly well equipped to deal with such singularity. In short, I decided that the best course of action would be to treat Aphro just like anyone else.

(expedition finances)

I had long been toying with the idea of employing a maid, having calculated that I was spending on average five hours a week cooking and cleaning for myself, whilst at the same time paying a man called Trumperton, who devoted perhaps half that length of time to managing my investments, a sum so exorbitant that for the sake of convenience it was expressed to the nearest thousand pounds.

So far as I could tell this sum was index-linked. The index was generated by calculating the quarterly cost of a not altogether notional *average Trumperton shopping basket*, which, amongst many, many other items, included three sets of boarding-school fees, repayments on the hefty Trumperton mortgage, wages for one live-in nanny, two two-week holidays in the sun for six, and, once a year, when the new registration plates came out, a very large, very heavy, very fast English-built sports saloon of a marque for which Trumperton had a weakness that bordered upon mania. The price of this average Trumperton shopping basket was divided between his clients in proportion to their wealth, and the appropriate sums were extracted from their accounts.

I will not accuse him of outright cupidity, for to give him his due, Trumperton was not wholly a stranger to that stoical indifference to money that for thousands of years was regarded by many as a sign of true nobility of spirit. I say so only because he managed my investments with a singular lack of flair, and really seemed to believe that capital growth, like the growth of flowers and foals and affection, was a thing which in no circumstances should be forced. Moreover, despite the enormous sums of money he helped himself to from my fortune, his attitude remained dry and unemotional at all times. Gratitude was not a button on his calculator.

Yet, whenever I attempted to raise the subject of his lacklustre results, his arched eyebrows and distastefully pursed lips suggested that, in attempting to link performance to reward, it was I who was breaching the age-old English gentleman's pact to act as if money means nothing; I who was the sordid, talentless shyster plumping my brood at the expense of innocent rich folk; I who flouted day after day the age-old taboo against money-grubbing.*

---

* Erratum: My publishers have since informed me that, to their

The previous year Trumperton's fees had been greater than the after-tax profit on my portfolio, and our relationship had fallen to a new low. As he, Trumperton, enriched himself, I, Otto, was impoverished. When the value of my investments fell, Trumperton excused himself on the grounds that we were in a bear market. Yet when the value of those same investments rose, Trumperton was the first to congratulate himself on his analytical and predictive brilliance.

Looking further into the subject, I had discovered that several learned economists had researched the problem in depth, and arrived at the conclusion that stockmarkets are perfectly unpredictable, and that a monkey with a pin would do as good a job as the most well-informed, diligent, profit-hungry, and even, dare I say it, *intelligent* investment manager.

I do not repeat this finding here because of any irrational prejudice in favour of other primates. I'm fond of human beings, and if city analysts, investment advisers and the like demanded nothing more than a bunch of bananas to keep them on the job, there would be no competition. Unfortunately, they do not: they charge in accordance with the cost of an average Trumperton shopping basket, an index that measures the quantity of

---

professional knowledge, this taboo no longer operates. Apologies for this factual inaccuracy.

needless luxuries the average middleclass lout can have delivered to his home in a year.

So it was that, upon meeting Aphro and finding myself moved by the almost sublimely disinterested idea of supporting her in her academic career, the notion of simultaneously taking hold of my own financial destiny crystallized in my mind. I was presented with a choice: I could dust and vacuum my flat, while Trumperton or another of his ilk sucked on my fortune as upon a boiled sweet, eking out the pleasure, neither chewing nor swallowing, until its substance was finally absorbed into his own flesh; or else I could employ a maid and take on the easy work myself.

Aphro seemed ideal. In her time off from studying she would easily be able to do the small amount of housework it took to keep my genuine loft-style apartment* habitable, leaving me free to engage in the tricky task of sticking pins in the Companies and Markets section of the *Financial Times* and phoning the results through to my broker. If I underperformed Chimp-Trumperton by less than 2½ per cent per annum (plus whatever sum Aphro demanded for her services), then I would break even; anything better and I would be in

---

* How it can be both *genuine* and at the same time *in the style of* a loft raises a question of nomenclature that I am not qualified to answer. But it is a good size, and centrally located.

profit. The Trumperton-Chimplets may have to suffer the humiliation of being dropped off at school in last year's millionaire-mover, but adversity is widely acknowledged to be a great educator,[*] and all in all I couldn't help thinking that, on balance, the general good would be better served by sacking Trumperton and hiring Aphro.

My mind made up, I placed regular orders for the *FT* and *The Investor's Chronicle*, faxed a leading theatrical costumier for a box of pins,[†] and made a beeline for the nearest all-night grocers, to stock up on bananas.

---

[*] Albeit generally by those who have not suffered it themselves.
[†] The type with brightly coloured plastic beads for heads, which I chose on the grounds that, since I did not know when it might become necessary for me to delegate my work, I should select tools well suited to operation by the lower primates, who might have difficulties in grasping the steel-tipped variety.

(building a team)

As I had promised, I phoned Aphro the morning after our first meeting. We seemed to be on an exceptionally clear line, even for a local call, and from her very first word I could hear every subtlety of her intonation and breathing. It was as though the room was filled by her voice, and I were seeing her face in big close-up.

FADE IN:

INT. APHRO'S BEDSIT - DAWN

It is very early. Aphro is tucked up in bed, sound asleep. Otto is on tenterhooks. The phone rings. Aphro turns on her bedside lamp (Ikea) and picks up.

          APHRO
     Huhluh?

OTTO (OFF-SCREEN)
Aphro, it's Otto.

APHRO
Otto?

OTTO (OFF-SCREEN)
Otto.

APHRO
(happily)
Ugh.

Aphro checks the time.

INT. OTTO'S GENUINE LOFT-STYLE APARTMENT - DAWN

From his vantage point on the seventeenth floor
of this exclusive apartment block Otto gazes
calmly at the waking city, a half-smile playing
on his lips. The sky is clear, the dawning sun
a reddish gold, and the Palace of Westminster
looks like an overdecorated wedding cake.

OTTO
Aphro?

APHRO (OFF-SCREEN)
Otto . . . it's six thirty.

>   OTTO
> Sorry. Were you asleep?

INT. APHRO'S CELL - DAWN

There is barely room to swing a cat.

>   APHRO
> Uh . . . yuh.

>   OTTO (OFF TO A BAD START)
> Sorry. I'll ring back later.

>   APHRO
> Nuh . . . nuh . . . wait.

Aphro puts down the receiver, slips out of bed, puts on her dressing gown, and endeavours to wake herself up.

INT. 4862 SQUARE FEET - DAWN

In a masterly show of indifference, Otto twitches slightly, while stamping his left foot in order to prevent his leg from shaking. A moment later, for no apparent reason, he flings himself onto a nearby sofa.

INT. 294 SQUARE FEET - DAWN

APHRO
(speaking in a calm, soothing tone - surprisingly self-possessed for a woman who
is about to be reduced to a condition of
humiliating domestic servitude)
What can I do for you, Otto?

INT. DESIGNED - DAWN

OTTO
(briskly)
Five hours of chores a week, to include
cleaning, ironing, and cooking, together
with the occasional errand, such as shopping. You'll have your own bedroom and bathroom. You won't be required to clean in my
bedroom or bathroom, or to enter them for
any other purpose. You will live rent-free.
Food and bills will be included in the pack-
age. Your salary will be paid weekly or
monthly, according to your preference.

INT. A SUPERIOR MIND - DAY

APHRO
(laughing)
And what about the salary? I mean, five hours
of my time a week must be worth, oh, at least
fifty thousand a year.

EXT. INT. - NIGHT (MOVING)

> OTTO
> (deadpan)
> As I said yesterday, in order to avoid dis-
> putes, and to set our relationship on the
> right footing, I think we should link your
> pay to one of the more senior grades in the
> civil service. Money means nothing to me.

> APHRO (OFF-SCREEN)
> Precisely nothing, or more or less nothing?

Otto furrows his brow.

> OTTO
> More or less nothing.

INT. APHRO'S HOVEL - IN ALL LIKELIHOOD OWNED BY
THE CREEP WHO RUNS THE LAUNDERETTE DOWNSTAIRS

Aphro is smiling, making herself a cup of tea.

> APHRO
> Otto . . .

> OTTO (OFF-SCREEN LEFT)
> Aphro?

>   APHRO
>   You're completely mad. I like you, and I
>   don't mean to be rude, but your behaviour is
>   utterly bizarre.

Otto rushes round to the other side of the
screen.

>   OTTO (OFF-SCREEN RIGHT)
>   That's my business.

>   APHRO
>   What, you mean you do it professionally?

INT. OTTO'S GENUINE LOFT-STYLE APARTMENT -
SPARSELY FURNISHED WITH A MIXTURE OF TWENTIETH-
CENTURY DESIGN CLASSICS (EAMES BEING PARTICU-
LARLY WELL REPRESENTED) AND EXCEPTIONALLY
TASTEFUL ANTIQUES - ALL IN ALL AN EXQUISITE BLEND
OF SENSIBILITY AND RAW FINANCIAL MUSCLE.

>   OTTO
>   (half shouting, half sobbing)
>   You know very well that's not what I mean.

>   APHRO
>   Sorry.

> OTTO
>
> I'm sorry. I'm not normally bad tempered. It's
> just that I've been up all night . . . working.

New angle on Otto, his ashen face partially
reflected in a mirror on a nearby coffee table.
The mirror is covered with white powder. Next to
the mirror is a plastic bag half-full of the same
white powder, together with a razor blade and a
twenty pound note rolled to form a tube. Through
the powder Otto's face looks insubstantial,
other-worldly, ghostlike.

> APHRO
> (dubiously)
> I see . . .
> (beat)
> Well, look, why don't we get together and
> . . . discuss it?

> OTTO
> OK, fine. Where?

> APHRO
> Somewhere . . . public.

> OTTO
> How about the whispering gallery in St
> Paul's?

APHRO

How about a pub or a café?

OTTO

Fine.
    (jungle beat)
How about lunch?

There is another pause. Otto exudes something of
the forced calmness of a man who is about to mount
the scaffold.

APHRO

Well . . .

OTTO
    (rather aggressively)
Don't imagine for a second that I'm making
this offer with anything other than the
loftiest intentions.

APHRO

Otto, imagination doesn't come into it,
you've beggared mine already. Listen, I'll
see you this evening at the Old Red Lion.
It's half a mile up the road from the bar
where we met. I'll see you there at six. I'll
have to leave at seven.

OTTO
Fine, I'll cancel my entire diary and see
you there.

APHRO
Otto . . .

Otto presses the 'end call' button and flings his
cordless handset across the room. It hits a beautiful white urn, the broad, curvaceous base of
which is strongly suggestive of the flesh-
quilted pelvis of a woman of child-bearing age.
The urn shatters. The phone rebounds off the
wall, falls to the floor and, curiously, begins
to ring. Crawling over to it on his hands and
knees, as if desperately attempting to extricate himself from a tunnel that is collapsing
behind him - cutting himself rather badly on
shards of porcelain in the process - Otto grabs
the phone and takes the call. It is his answering
service.

DIGITALLY SIMULATED FEMALE VOICE
(Patronizing tone)
You have *no* new messages.

In the west the fury of the day subsides.

FADE OUT.

(philosophy of filth)

So it became clear to me that Aphro wouldn't easily be swayed by the innumerable advantages I could offer her. Confused and hurt to find my altruistic impulses greeted with such disdain, I decided not to keep my date with Aphro, and sat down to write the following letter, explaining my decision.

Dear Aphro,

Following our phone call this morning, I am writing to tell you that I am no longer considering you for the vacancy I invited you to apply for. While I have no doubts about your general abilities and your eminent suitability for the role as advertised, I find myself reluctantly obliged to acknowledge that a total absence of venality in an employee can cause great practical difficulties. It is in this respect that I have come to believe you are lacking.

As Aristotle says, the virtuous person follows the

mean in all things. Where money is concerned, this means that virtue bids us take a middle course between avarice and profligacy. Whereas a person who can't remember from day to day whether they've got large sums of free cash or are crippled by debt – the sort of person who wouldn't be crippled by debt, because without batting an eyelid they'd simply go and ask a friend for a loan, who would immediately give them all the money they needed, such is the love and loyalty that person habitually inspires in those close to them – that sort of person can be extremely difficult to manage effectively. For such a person can only be motivated by beauty, goodness, the desire to see others flourish, etcetera – all qualities that are difficult to feign. When faced with such an employee, an employer who possesses none of these so-called 'higher' qualities is faced with no choice but to resort to dishonesty, dissimulation, and manipulation.

The father of psychoanalysis,* Sigmund Freud, famously maintained that the irrational disgust some people feel towards money, and the irrational love felt by others, is explained by the equation that exists in the infantile imagination between money and faeces, which as babies we regard as our most prized possession and which, like money, can equally well be given away as a present or kept for our own pleasure and amusement.

---

* Psycho-anal-ism: a reductive account of the human spirit in terms of the human arse.

The story goes that people whose passionate attachment to their faeces never truly fades will have an excessive love of money too, whereas people who are over-fastidious about faeces develop a similar diffidence or even repulsion towards 'filthy' lucre.

The analogy is a striking one, for money is an essential by-product of economic activity. Conversely, if you do not shit, sooner or later you will find yourself unable to ingest further nutrition, and in much the same way economic growth depends upon a healthy move-ment of money through the body politic.

Yet there is an even more compelling disanalogy. For, as Cervantes gleefully points out in *Don Quixote*, shitting is the one thing that no one else can do for you; whereas, as Defoe amply demonstrates in *Robinson Crusoe*, being rich is one of the few things that no one can do alone.

So allow me to take another tack: experimental psychologists have proved that people only become repelled by their own excrements once they are separated from them,* and it seems to me that this psycho-logical phenomenon provides the more likely expla-nation for your feelings of queasiness. For is money not precisely what is left over when the world has been stripped of all its nutritional properties? As food is

---

* When offered a glass of their own spittle to drink, a surprising (?) number of subjects declined the offer, though they swallow pints of the stuff every day.

reduced to ordure, so land, sea, sky, labour, art, ingenuity, beauty and ultimately life itself are reduced to that simple numerical relation we call money. Some people are disgusted by this process of digestion, whilst for others money becomes the ideal, universal, eternal object of desire.

Alternatively, taking as our starting point the notion of money as the universal object of desire, cut to the reverse angle and we immediately see that, far from giving us the power to possess the world, money is the cause of our final separation from it. For, whilst for some a healthy bank balance may represent a store of joy just waiting to be unleashed, is there a single one of those pleasures, a single one of those much cherished possessions, which cannot just as effectively be re-converted into the same glistening dung from whence it appeared to originate? Yes, we are mathematical Midases, we moderns. We no more than look at a thing of worth than it is converted into its numerical equivalent. It can happen at any time, to any kind of object. It can even happen to people – even to you, Aphro.

The technical term for this process is *liquidation*. Do not attempt to resist the process of liquidation, Aphro: to do so will only cause pain and embarrassment. Ashes to ashes, dust to dust, Aphro.

I may have read you wrongly, of course. One often finds that, far from lacking that moderate degree of cupidity of which Aristotle, Aquinas, Austen, et al. would have approved, people like yourself, who seem indifferent towards money, and who even affect to despise it, actually have a greed of gain so profound, a pride of financial 'independence' so distended, that what seems on the surface to be a heartfelt abhorrence for a person who has been so base as to make a cash offer is in reality a wholesome contempt towards the sum offered, which is far too small. In other words, it was not the fact that an offer was made but the sum itself that offended.

To conclude, a human being who scorns money is no more use than a gardener who scorns manure.

Even so, I do appreciate that you have more to offer than most in the current employment market, and am willing to consider increasing my initial offer, by up to 100 per cent if necessary.

Yours sincerely,

Otto

Having clarified my feelings, I decided not to send the letter after all, which I thought of an excessively technical nature, and liable to give the wrong impression of my own interests and character. Instead I decided I would explain myself to Aphro in person at the Old Red Lion. It was 9.30 a.m., so I cleaned my teeth, took a moderate overdose of sedatives, set my alarm clock for 4.30 p.m., and retired to bed.

(ethical tourism)

At around midday I had the misfortune to prematurely resume* consciousness.† Staggering about in my dressing gown, wondering vaguely who I was and whether I should care, it took me around an hour to prepare and consume a triple espresso and a croissant, after which gustatory debacle I felt marginally more integrated.

It was an unprecedentedly blue day. The tide was high and, like the hypocritical murderer who sheds a tear at the funeral of his victim, even the canker-coloured Thames had taken on an obscure hint of azure. I watched the current pulling at the piles beneath the bridges. It pulled and pulled and pulled, yet neither

---

* I am often amazed by the failure of even the strongest narcotics to quell my seemingly irrepressible *joie de vivre*.
† A jocular term designating that condition of purposeless activity characteristic of human beings who are temporarily neither sleeping nor dead.

Embankment nor Waterloo Bridge was destroyed whilst I was watching. This seemed a good omen, and was a comfort to me. And neither did the bloated corpses of any west London or Buckinghamshire suicides float by, which likewise seemed to augur well for the day. I felt as if poised on a very sharp yet extraordinarily comfortable knife-edge. Without wanting to brag, I think it's fair to say that the evidence strongly suggested that my mood was exultant. A little less Temazepam in my system and I'd have known for sure.

The phone rang – the self-same phone that I had accidentally dropped earlier in the day. I chuckled to myself, charmed by the pertinacity of modern telecommunication; I felt towards that phone as one who has a soft-spot for vicious, fetid, sharp-clawed furry animals might feel towards a mink, or a civet, or a fox. It didn't stop ringing, so after about five minutes I picked it up.

'What are you up to, you sewer rat?'

It was Max.

'Hello, you're through to Otto's answerphone. If you'd like to leave a message, please do so after the bleep,' I said. Then I made a beeping sound. Unbelievably, Max bought it. 'Otto, you're a creep. You're attempting to take on one of my most brilliant students as a skivvy. Domestic servitude is demeaning, both to the servant and the served. Why should one person be forced by reason of economic deprivation to tend to the bodily needs of another – especially someone like you? I know you, Otto; you're doing this on purpose in order to humiliate Aphro because you're threatened by her intelligence. And ultimately you're doing it in order to get at me. Don't think I don't see all this. Ring me back, you inky little squid.'

'Max, how charming to hear from you,' I replied, somewhat blearily.

'Oh, you're there, are you?'

'Yes, I was pretending to be my answerphone. It was a joke.'

'Very funny.'

'Don't worry, you'll probably find yourself laughing later on in your development, once you've reached the stage where humour becomes possible. It comes after the capacity for spatial reasoning, which I know you've already reached, because you spend so much time with your foot in your mouth.' What I've just said sounds vaguely funny to me, but Max doesn't laugh at all. I suspect this is because I said it far too slowly, as a result of the Temazepam, so that all the goodness seeped out of the words as I was saying them.

Max seems to think so too, because the next thing he asks me is, 'What have you been taking, Otto? You sound like an educationally retarded sloth.'

'Hang on, Max, someone's on the other line,' I say as rapidly as I can. Then I put down the receiver, stumble across the room, cut and snort a fat line of speed, and pick up the phone again, now moving with a Howitzer-sized spring in my step. 'Sorry. Got rid of them. What can I do for you?'

'You're a savage, Otto – a real barbarian.'

'It's strange, but your voice sounds somehow . . . pre-recorded – as if I've heard this message before . . .'

'Don't give me that. What are you playing at?'

'Max, with the amount of money I have, it would be immoral not to have a maid. I'm doing exactly what you would do if, God forbid, you were ever allowed to run the country: I'm creating employment. You should be congratulating me. There's no reason to think Aphro will be debased. She won't have to make love to me; she only has to look after me a bit – shopping and cooking and doing the laundry and that sort of thing . . .'

'And cleaning,' interjected Max.

'Yes, and cleaning. What's wrong with that? I've cleaned for myself for long enough to know it does no harm. I've even cleaned for you when you've stayed in my flat, though you probably don't remember – you certainly never thanked me for it. So why shouldn't I pay someone to clean for me? I need to free up time for other things.'

'Like what?' demanded Max rudely. 'You're the most under-occupied person I know.'

'Like looking after my investments,' I said, sounding so sincere now that I was teetering on the verge of believing myself. 'I'm not satisfied with the performance of my portfolio manager, so I've decided to take charge of things myself.'

'So that you can ensure that you only invest in companies that squeeze every last drop of unpaid labour out of their workforces, whilst at the same time minimizing pay and benefits, and extorting every last penny from their customers by pursuing monopoly or cartel control over their markets, and reducing the force of environmental and consumer-protection legislation by manipulating the decision-making processes of democratic governments and relocating factories to countries where such legislation doesn't yet exist ... in order to line your own already-bulging pockets all the more effectively? So that what? So that you can take on *another* maid? Get a life, you sad bastard.'

At this point, Max and I launched into one of our set-piece arguments. Without reporting the conversation in full, which would be tedious even to me, I probably ought to explain that Max has been duped by an antiquated economic theory that holds that economic value does not exist until a human being does some work. According to this theory, money is crystallized labour, and making a profit requires that the employer should extract more work from the employee than is represented in money-form by their wages. In other words, profit is stolen or extorted labour.

As far as I could tell, Max expounded this theory mainly in order to make me feel guilty. My reasoning was that, deep down, Max was a miserable man. I, on the other hand, was sublimely happy – often almost hysterically so. It is only when a man comes across a genuinely happy, smiling face that he realizes just how unhappy he himself is, and I was convinced that Max's moral and intellectual mission in life was to make everyone who is happy feel bad about themselves in order to reduce the painful contrast that would otherwise exist between himself and them. In short, he had convinced himself that if he could only abolish life's peaks, the trough which he inhabited might come to seem a little less dark, dank and miserable.

I didn't believe Max's theory. These days, people pay more for what *hasn't* been done than what has. Mankind's economic activities turn gold into lead everywhere we look. Fresh air, for instance – if there is anything left on the planet that fits that description – trades at a premium.

My view was that, far from being crystallized labour, value is a function of a far more noble quality – that is, rarity. Rarity can be created or destroyed by a change in the weather, and is as likely to pertain to an empty space or even a vacuum, as it is to something that has purposely been manufactured. The first rule of economics is, if one has control of something rare, one will be able to get money for it.* Apples, for instance, are seldom found outside shops and cafeterias, and for this reason alone business-swindlers – and swindleresses – are able to charge money for them; whereas, in those areas of the world where they grow on trees, they are generally available free of charge.

I argued along these lines with Max for some time, he putting his rose-tinted leftist view, while I countered his arguments with my self-serving and no less dishonest liberal version. After a while Max had almost forgotten about Aphro's existence.

'You're a sly old fox,' said Max at last, as our debate drew to a close and Max discovered that, while his knowledge of economics was far deeper than my own, he had failed to get the better of me and that, what was more, he had been successfully diverted from his real concern, which was the moral welfare of his favourite student.

'Why, thank you, Max,' I said, gracefully acknowledg-

---

* This doesn't hold true in the cases of rare diseases, of course, nor of unusual birth defects; the second rule of economics is that people have to want whatever it is. And the third is, they have to be able to pay for it.

ing the compliment. What Max has yet to realize, bless him, is that white lies are intrinsically no more convincing than black ones. Indeed, they are usually far less so, for it seldom takes much effort to make people believe the worst, concerning which most people have had far more hands-on experience than its opposite.

Returning to his purpose at last, Max half-heartedly threatened to tell Aphro that I had a dubious sexual history and was a notorious dope fiend. At this point I took the liberty of laughing in his face, whilst gently reminding him of certain photographs I had in my possession.

His pathetic effort at blackmail outstripped by my own turbo-charged version, Max then took a stab at raw humiliation, demanding that I should tell him whether I would get a sexual frisson from 'barking orders' at a beautiful young woman. And I have to admit that this question did shake me. Because, to borrow a line from one of my great fictional heroes, I am, if I may be permitted to say so, the least arrogant creature that ever walked God's earth. The idea of giving orders to a fellow human being – let alone barking them – filled me with genuine horror; the idea that I might obtain some kind of pleasure from doing so was loathsome to me.

'She will only be required to work in the communal areas of the flat. She will choose her own working hours, set her own tasks, and be judged in her performance of those tasks by no one but herself,' I declared.

'You're a freak, Otto,' said Max. There was a significant pause. 'If you fancy her, why don't you just ask her out for a drink or something?'

'Max,' I declared, 'you're obsessed with sex. It's sad. Listen to yourself.'

'I know,' chuckled Max.

Got him!

After this delicate, unexpected *épée* thrust, Max's rhetoric fell limp, and our conversation ended soon afterwards. He had been forced to acknowledge that the real reason why he was becoming heated about the whole thing was that he wanted to get into Aphro's knickers. Typical pedagogue! Snob that he was, he would find it humiliating to have a relationship with my maid.

Even so, he could not leave me without a parting shot. 'If you believe that all people are equal,' he pronounced, 'you should have no truck with such an arrangement – especially not with a woman of Aphro's calibre.'

'But I don't believe that all people are equal, Max; some are far, far better than others.'

'Then you're a bastard,' he said.

'Not a bastard, an orphan,' I corrected him.

Got him again!

He was speechless. When we finally said goodbye, Max was two-nil down. It was three o'clock in the afternoon. The sun was still shining. I took this as yet another favourable portent, and decided to go for a drive.

(a journey by road)

A journey by road is, for many people, the most authentic taste they ever have of truly independent travel. Put petrol in your tank, oil in your sump, tread on your tyres and amps in your battery, and you will be ready to move, helter-skelter, on the vector of your own choosing, stopping and starting as and when you like, accelerating and decelerating as conditions and/or your mood dictates; opening and closing the windows, turning the CD player on and off, up and down, fiddling with the climate-control system, making in-car phone calls ... the possibilities are endless.

In an age of almost infinite freedom of consumer choice, deciding on what vehicle to buy can be a vexed question. Basically, the main choice lies between fast cars, slow cars, and off-road vehicles, which themselves can be either fast or slow.

Four-wheel drive enables one to shrug off the narrow

restrictions of the metalled road system, heading out across open country whenever one wishes. This is especially useful when the motorways and A-roads are blocked by queues of vehicles – an increasingly prevalent and irritating problem, as the attractions of independent travel grow greater year by year, and vast hordes of people take to exercising their freedom to drive in exactly the same direction at precisely the same times of day and night. This ability to jump queues by taking to the fields explains what would otherwise be the irrational preponderance of massively heavy, fuel-guzzling, fume-spewing four-wheel-drive vehicles one sees on the streets of London – which are, it is perhaps worthwhile pointing out for the benefit of anyone who has not been there since the nineteenth century, paved and pavemented to the last inch.

After the question of two- or four-wheel drive has been decided, the remaining choice lies between fast cars and slow. My friend Max always insists that there could be no imaginable justification for owning a high-performance sports car when you live in a city in which the average speed of the traffic has not increased since the days of horse-drawn carriages. The extra fuel that a vehicle with a large, powerful engine uses is an affront to anyone who values the future of mankind, and the extra pollution caused by burning this fuel is an affront to the millions of men, women, and children who are forced to inhale its sooty, sulphurous, carbon-monox-ious byproducts of combustion.

My opinion was rather different. As it happened, I owned a rather nippy piece of kit myself. And, while it was true that I seldom reached its top speed of 161 m.p.h., it was nevertheless capable of whisking me through gaps in the traffic, propelling me out of side-streets, and catapulting me past slower vehicles on straight sections of road so short that owners of lower-performance vehicles would probably describe them as hairpin bends. Furthermore, while I was a great respecter of people's right to roam, and even to cross roads when necessary, a high-performance car such as the one I owned enables one to inflict from a standing start the sort of injuries that the driver of a more modest vehicle can only achieve with a run-up. And although I sincerely hoped never to be forced to utilize my car's capability in this respect, when an antisocial type was lingering aggressively on a pedestrian crossing, hindering the free flow of traffic, it was comforting to know that the means of retribution lay comfortably within my power.

But Max had a point: London is abysmally congested, pedestrians show very little respect for any but the most erratically driven vehicles, parking is a nightmare, the air is foul, and the health of your children is suffering.* The

---

* I took the precaution of not having any.

solution I chose was a compromise (and what aspect of our lives, in this day and age, is not scored, scarred, and riven with such compromises?). Namely, I chose to own a fabulously fast and powerful Italian sports car, which as a rule I only removed from its underground car-parking bay in order to have it serviced. This saved on fuel bills, helped to keep the environment clean, and kept Max off my back, while at the same time giving me the pleasure of owning a brilliantly engineered, futuristic, flame-red, V12, turbo-charged supercar – a powerful symbol of my masculinity and my social status, and an enormous pleasure to drive.

And if I chose to do so, on average, only once or twice a year, that did not detract from the fact that, by having the vehicle close to hand and ready to roll, I was free to set off whenever and wherever I pleased. Within ten or twenty or perhaps thirty hours, should the urge take me, I could be pulling up outside a casino in Monaco, taking the drag lift to the top of a favourite black run near Cortina, chomping caviar in a Petersburg restaurant, or snuggling down in a motorway hotel room somewhere outside Birmingham (traffic permitting).

It took me half an hour to find my car keys, during which time I gulped down two mugs of hot, soothingly milky tea.

I should perhaps have counted the mislaying of my

keys as an unfavourable augur and scored it against the foregoing favourable ones, as they do with votes in democratic assemblies. Had I done so, I would no doubt have chosen to stay put where I was. But the amphetamines I had taken were counterbalancing the barbiturates so delicately, and had consequently brought my metabolism and subjective psychological state to such a pitch of perfection – the mean, as it were, between the two extremes of soaring and slumping – that my mood was almost indistinguishable from that condition I believe people are referring to when they say they are feeling 'all right' or even 'normal'.* And I found this feeling both unfamiliar and somewhat distracting.

So it was, perhaps, that the traveller in me began itching to take to the road – to escape the trivial concerns that were weighing me down, concerns that can submerge a man's soul as spirit vinegar submerges a young cucumber or gherkin, gradually seeping into the flesh, penetrating the free, fresh, proud, upstanding, self-reliant, self-determining, experience-hungry, carefree, questing, independent bundle of unalloyed energy and enthusiasm that a man, essentially, in himself, and by nature, is and ought to be, thus transforming him

---

* Though without any of the demeaning dependency on circumstantial factors which that word implies.

into something domesticated, bottled, and rather acidic, like Max.

Yes, the Nietzschean *Übermensch* in me was aching to express himself, and I was feeling reckless. And so it was that, at three-thirty in the afternoon, I walked* the short distance from my flat to the underground car park where I kept my vehicle – savouring the sunshine, the refreshing breeze, the extra inches of flesh that were being displayed by the female office workers who all the time patter this way and that along the Embankment – looking forward to feeling the wind in my hair and watching the open road unfold before me, as the map of my destiny might unfurl in some delightful dream. I descended to the second level, found my car (parked conveniently near to the pedestrian exit), unlocked the padlock on the little barrier that prevents people from parking in my space, and climbed aboard.

Shortly afterwards, the seeds of disaster were sown.† Intoxicated as I was – first of all by the brilliance of the day, secondly by the combined effect of the smell and texture of my leather upholstery, my precariously low-slung driving position, the brilliant red of my bodywork, my flared wheel arches, my aggressive radiator fins and, last but by no means least, the rasping battle cry of my

---

* In classical terms, the *anabasis*.
† The *protasis*.

twin exhausts – I pulled out of my parking space without taking the necessary precautions.*

Turning right, I accelerated up to around 27 m.p.h. (first gear), took the steeply angled spiral connecting ramp to level one at a leisurely 17 m.p.h. (first gear), rocketed up to 35 m.p.h. on level one's first straight, took the notoriously tight double right-hander into the second straight at a tyre-squeelingly nifty 23 m.p.h. (first gear), before taking the single right-hander back on to the ramp, which (the rubber of my tyres being by now somewhat warmer and grippier) I took at a breathtaking 25 m.p.h. (first gear). Peeling out of the bend and into the short straight that leads to the exit barrier – and the brilliance of the late-afternoon sunshine – I accelerated up to 39 m.p.h. (first gear) before coming to a gut-pluckingly abrupt halt, my windscreen only inches away from the car-park entrance barrier.† At this point, I took out my wallet (waterproof and highly durable reverse nubuck chinchilla skin with a 24-carat gold clasp) only

---

*   As with any tragedy, my initial slip was separated in time from its inevitable and crushing consequence. Traditionally, as the hero careers towards his *catastrophe*, the audience, who knows exactly what will ensue, savours the superior pleasures of dramatic irony. Frankly, I fail to see why I should put myself at such a disadvantage; you'll find out what I had done wrong when it is too late to do anything about it, just as I did.

†   Thus concluding the *epistasis*.

to discover that I had neglected to bring my plastic ID pass with me.*

Never one to be defeated by misfortune, I decided to attempt to drive directly underneath the barrier. I had often suspected that my exceptionally ground-hugging vehicle might well have a sufficiently low clearance to allow me to drive underneath the red and yellow striped arm without stopping; now was the time to find out. I edged the vehicle forwards (first gear), watching with bated breath as the bar moved slowly past my wind-screen, which was so aerodynamically efficient as to be virtually horizontal. When it had disappeared entirely from view I stopped the car for a moment, took a deep breath, steeled my nerves, then began edging forwards once more. Two seconds later an unpleasant grating sound reverberated throughout the cabin.

I stopped the car and attempted to open the door in order to check out the damage. But the machine through which the privileged owners of annual parking permits must swipe their plastic cards was in the way, and I was forced to move from the driver's seat to the passenger seat in order to exit on the other side.

Extricating yourself from an ultra-low, hip-hugging bucket seat and clambering over the extremely high transmission tunnel without becoming snagged or

---

* And so passing seamlessly into the *catastasis*.

impaled upon the gearstick, before slotting yourself in the equally ultra-low hip-hugging bucket seat where one's passenger (if one were to take passengers; I myself did not) would sit, is a tricky business at the best of times. Unfortunately, on this occasion, just as I was straddling the transmission tunnel, having been forced to adopt a crab-like posture that was somewhat sexually suggestive, if not downright lewd, someone appeared behind me and tooted their horn.

The surprise produced in me by this unexpected clarion-blast caused me to slip backwards, forcing the stubby, red-tipped gearstick* painfully into the extremely sensitive area of flesh† that lies between the anus and the scrotum – more or less where, if I had one (and presuming I was constructed along normal lines), my vagina would be. The unwelcome stabbing sensation caused by this intrusion caused me to buck and twitch in such agony that, when I finally emerged from the passenger door, I felt sure that the man in the car behind me must be convinced that I had been putting on some sort of erotic show for him.

Already deeply embarrassed, and forced by the bruising beneath my scrotum to walk with a very uncharacteristic swagger, I approached the vastly oversized, vastly

---

*   The *catachresis*.
†   The *perineum*.

overpowered, city-camouflaged, Korean-built business assault vehicle. A window slid silently down and I found myself face-to-face with a savvy-looking businessmale, who asked me, with one potent gesture of an eyebrow, exactly what the trouble was and if he could help.

I explained, with maximum insouciance – as though it were really an ordinary everyday sort of thing – that, having forgotten my pass, I had been attempting to limbo beneath the barrier when my vehicle had unexpectedly become stuck. He laughed long and hard. It took me a while to convince him that if he lent me his card he would not become locked inside the garage himself, but eventually I managed to wrest the crucial piece of plastic from his grip and operated the barrier with it. Without stopping to check the damage, I ran around to the passenger door of my car, jumped in, clambered painfully across the transmission tunnel (this time performing the manoeuvre 'doggy-style'), slithered into the driver's seat, turned the keys in the ignition, waited for the engine to burst into life, and was just about to push the threateningly pert gearstick into first (first) gear when the barrier came scything down on the roof with an embarrassing (and potentially expensive) clonk.

Without turning off the engine, I lowered the driver's-side window and attempted with my left hand to reach far enough backwards and upwards to ease the plastic card into the slot once more. But my arm was too short.

I did not struggle for long, however, because a moment later the aforesaid kind businessgentleman arrived in person in order to help me out. No longer laughing, he snatched the card from my hand and rather tersely stated his intention to sort the situation out. He operated the barrier. Without looking back, or even acknowledging the man's help (although chivalrous at first his attitude, I thought, had latterly grown churlish), I accelerated towards the open road, hitting a maximum speed of 10 m.p.h. (first gear) before coming to rest at the 'Give Way' sign.

Looking carefully each way before pulling out I turned left into the street, accelerated up to the legal speed limit of 30 m.p.h. (0–30 m.p.h., 1.4 secs; first gear), took the ninety-degree 'Bagel Shop Corner' (a left-hander) without touching my brakes, as I fought valiantly to make up those vital seconds I had let slip at the exit barrier.* Continuing at 30 m.p.h. (first gear) for the next ten or fifteen feet, I then slammed on the anchors, dropping down to around 7 m.p.h. for 'Car Park This Way, Pay on Exit' corner (a treacherously tight left-hander with reverse camber; first gear). I powered out of the bend and back up to around 20 m.p.h. (first gear) down the short incline that leads directly to the spiral entrance ramp, which I took flat out all the

---

* Racing *à la recherche du temps perdu*, as they say in the *Renault* team.

way down to level two (29 m.p.h.; first gear; badly
scraped front bumper; lost nearside wing mirror). My
journey almost at its end – or so I thought – I then
accelerated up to a staggering 45 m.p.h. (first gear),
before squawking to a halt just before the pedestrian
exit. That's when the catastrophe came into view. Someone had parked in my space.

I had forgotten to put up the steel pillar.

It was not as if I had not been warned. The warden
had told me several times that I should keep it down
when I'm in and up when I'm out, the point being that
when your car is in its proper place it is not possible for
anyone else to park there, whereas when your car is out
it is only too easy for them to do so. The principle is
simple enough, and I do not see why I should not have
been able to grasp it. Yet time and time again I found
myself parking my loved one as close to the wall ahead
as possible, specifically in order that I might erect the
little column before abandoning her there. I wonder if I
was not fearful of theft? Or perhaps there was a nagging
doubt in my mind that, my car being so low to the
ground and so flat, some myopic motorist might one
day come along and park their car on top of it. Or
maybe I regarded the little column as a positional good,
and wished to have it raised, like a flag, to prove to
passers-by that the owner of the sexy red sports car had

enough spare cash to afford a private bay in this frighteningly expensive garage.

Whatever the psychological explanation, I had got it wrong again, and in my absence a turd-brown, 'small family' car had usurped my position. The sensible thing would have been to park my car elsewhere, erect my little steel pillar, padlock it, and leave a note of my phone number beneath the windscreen wiper of the offending vehicle, in order that they might ring me and beg to be released, when they finally returned from their whelking trip, or whatever it was that had brought them to the fertile banks of the Thames in the first place. But, sadly, they had not parked far back enough, and the steel pillar had become trapped beneath their vehicle.

Neither could I block their exit by parking directly in front of my space, for in doing so I would have prevented the owner of the space directly opposite mine from being able to remove his or her vehicle (a midsize German-built business assault vehicle). I had only two options left. Either I could park in a public space and return to the car park intermittently, once a day perhaps, possibly for several months, watching a succession of small family cars come and go until finally, due perhaps to petrol shortages or some other freak occurrence, my bay was liberated at last. Or I could park nearby, remain in my vehicle, and wait for the base pretenders to return to their vehicle. As the option most likely to save time in the long run, I chose the latter.

I parked in a facing bay, five spaces along from my own. In order to listen to my quadrophonic CD player for what could prove to be an extended stay without running the risk of draining my battery, I thought it safest to keep the engine of my car ticking over. Taking off my seatbelt, I settled down to listen to *Verklärte Nacht* by Arnold Schoenberg.* By the time the lachrymose ranks of shivering violins, violas, cellos, and double basses were building to their dire climax – as the woman in the poem first reveals her infidelity to her lover, then adds insult to injury by telling him that she has become pregnant by the other man – I had become so depressed that I fell asleep, missing altogether the tender if somewhat breathy reconciliation scene, in which the man (stupidly in my opinion) agrees to continue loving the woman, even going so far as to promise to love and cherish both her *and* the other man's child (yuck).

I awoke approximately two hours later with an extremely sore head. The car was, it is true, sitting in a dense cloud of exhaust fumes, and my window was, it is

---

* In the sumptuously miserable version for string orchestra by the LA Philharmonic, directed by Zubin Mehta. In my opinion, early Schoenberg is the pearl that grew around the romantic grit of Wagner and Brahms.

true, open to those fumes. Even so, I think it is more likely that the headache was the result of the Schoenberg CD, which I had accidentally left on 'repeat', than of carbon-monoxide poisoning.

But it wasn't the music that had woken me. The loving couple were still promenading in agony around the starlit garden (we were back once again at that dreadful moment when the woman reveals her shameful secret to her lover, blah, blah, blah). But this time the car had begun to tremble uncomfortably, as though overwhelmed by the drama of the music or, alternatively and more plausibly, as if one or two of the twelve richly lubricated designer cylinders was not working properly. I blipped the throttle by way of encouragement, and the engine responded by promptly dying on me. This I immediately recognized as the predictable consequence of any show of enthusiasm, good wishes, or affection on my part, and if I hadn't been half asleep, and half poisoned by Schoenberg's groundlessly optimistic *fin-de-siècle* bluster, I would never have attempted to intervene.

I tried the ignition a couple of times but the car was not to be revived. It was then I noticed that the petrol gauge was on empty. It seems I had run out of fuel. Turning off the CD, which I now disliked even more intensely than I had last time I spent all day listening to it, I looked up from the dashboard to see the offending brown vehicle cutting a swathe through the gradually dispersing cloud of wispy gray exhaust smoke. I stared, aghast.

As a length of pig's bowel is stuffed with veal, bacon and other tasty and nourishing ingredients to form an *andouillette*, and as a lifeboat is stuffed with women and children while the sinking ship takes the massed ranks of stiff-cocked, bowler-hatted gentlemen to the watery grave they had always foreseen for themselves and in many cases no doubt looked forward to with longing, so this vehicle was stuffed to bursting – with children, and with shopping, and with love. I started to cry.

I couldn't cry for long, however, for I had work to do. Releasing the handbrake and putting the gearbox in neutral, I leaped from the car and began trying to push it out of its temporary parking space and into the bay to which it was forsworn.

It is difficult to motivate manually a vehicle that is so exceptionally well adapted to coping with the extremes of mechanical force. Its aerodynamic lines offer very little purchase for the hands and, it being so low slung, one is obliged, if one is to put one's back into the job, to lean over until one is almost parallel to the ground – at which point it becomes extremely difficult to get one's shoes to grip the floor. Add to this the surprisingly effective resistance to movement, left or right, of the power-unassisted steering wheel (a direct consequence of the super-sticky, 24-inch-wide, low-profile front tyres, aggravated perhaps by my tendency to be rendered physically incompetent by even a brief exposure to emotion of any kind) and you have some idea of the difficulties I was up against.

Nevertheless I struggled manfully on, pushing the damned thing back and forth, utterly incapable of changing its direction. It behaved as if it was on rails. Everything behaved as if it was on rails. My entire life seemed suddenly so predictable that I felt for a moment that I must have come upon a straight section in space-time, and was gazing giddily into a far future which, sadly, was exactly the same as the present: I had always been in that car park and in that car park I would always remain. The car itself was a joke – a mere pretext; I didn't need it, I didn't use it – I didn't even like the way the damned thing looked. I was embarrassed to drive it through populous areas. The cabin was small and pokey, no good at all for having sex in. The high transmission tunnel made in-car fellatio with anyone other than a circus contortionist a physical impossibility, while the pink-tipped gearstick made it a rather dubious prop-osition merely on the grounds of strict logic.*

I began to doubt the existence of the external world. Not the world that is supposed somehow to be external to my mind, the existence of which philosophers have

---

* I refer of course to Leibniz's principle of the identity of indiscernibles.

doubted ever since Descartes came up with the idea in the first place; no, it was the existence of a world external to my car park that I was beginning to doubt. I stood beside my motorized oral-anal-genital phase and stared up at the low concrete ceiling. Was there, in truth, anything beyond it?

A car drove very quietly past me. It had to swerve a little to avoid me, but even so I took no notice of it. The ceiling was fascinating. Such an enigmatic gray colour; so ambiguously, so devastatingly colourless. And the smell of the place: steel, concrete, petrol and piss; the four humours of the city mingled into one rank odour. Could this be the smell of money? Was I locked inside a big, hollow coin? If so, what was its face value? Did it even have a face?

When I had done soliloquizing, I looked down from the ceiling just in time to see a besuited man disappear through the pedestrian exit. He looked exactly like a weasel disappearing through a hole. It was then I noticed that he had parked in my space.

When I finally ceased screaming my throat was sore, but I felt very calm.* Without even bothering to lock my vehicle, I left it where it was standing, half in and

---

* Nothing like a good *parabasis* when the comedy becomes too much for you.

half out of the parking space, and set off in pursuit of the slippery man.

By the time I reached the surface he was long gone. But at least I had made it to the surface. At least there was a surface. I began to feel grateful to him, even though he had stolen my space. For I felt sure I would never have reached the external world without him.

It was early evening. But we were well on our way to the solstice, and there was still plenty of sunshine left. Dishevelled, nauseated, and confused, I blinked at the daylight, trying to decide what to do. It was five o'clock, and I had to get to Islington by six. The sensible thing would have been to take a taxi to the nearest petrol station, buy a can of petrol, return to my vehicle, fill it up, drive to Islington, then return, and resume my vigil. But who was to say that the slippery man would return that evening? Who was to say he would ever return? Who was to say there would be any free spaces at all later in the evening? What would I do then? Sell my car to the parking attendant?

No, the thing was impossible. And anyway, the idea of going back into the car park filled me with dread. If I left the car as it was, the worst that could happen was that it would be stolen. Just so long as the thief did not leave the Schoenberg CD behind, I did not care.

I set off to walk to Islington.

On Blackfriars Bridge, an attractive, apparently sane

woman smiled at me as she passed. I was so surprised by this that I stopped in my tracks,* turned and stared. She never turned back. I watched as her figure receded into the distance, watched until it became an infinitely small but infinitely important dot in my visual field.

What had she seen?

---

* Or where my tracks would have been if I had been walking on mud rather than on paving stones, or if my feet had been bleeding.

(the lion rampant)

I arrived at the pub early. Apart from a few human beings, the place was empty. I bought a pint of beer – no, let's be specific, I bought a pint of stout. Then I played myself at pool and lost. I bought a second pint and played a return match. This time I played a little better, but due to a faint vibration in the pool cue, which was obviously defective, neither of us could get the black into any of the holes and the game ended in an honourable draw.

Aphro appeared, looking a little tired but exuding life. Since Sunday, her physical appearance was largely unaltered. I forget what it was, exactly, but roughly speaking the effect was either one of utter perfection or total corruption, depending on how frightened I was feeling. Certainly there was nothing middling about it. Aristotle would have disapproved.

'Been working?' I asked.

'Processing words,' she replied, with a grimace.

'You work in a canning factory?' I joked.

'Something like that.'

'Can I get you a drink?'

'Thanks, I'll have a tomato juice.'

'Oh, please,' I cajoled, indicating my glass, 'you'll make me feel bad about myself.'

'Tomato juice,' she replied, with an uncompromising smile.

'Crisps?'

'No thanks'

'Nuts?'

She shook her head.

'Crackling?' I ventured in desperation.

She laughed. 'No!'

I returned from the bar with a fresh pint for myself, and a double tomato juice without vodka for her.* Aphro was seated at a table, looking perfectly calm. I sat opposite her, and a little to one side, so as not to force her to stare at me if she didn't want to. She didn't.

'So,' I began cleverly, 'here we are ...'

'What's your game, Otto?' Aphro interrupted me, rather rudely I thought.

'Skiing mainly, but a little trekking, sailing, bungee-jumping, and the occasional undemanding Alpine

---

* Henceforth, let no woman say I do not respect female autonomy.

route,' I explained. 'You know the sort of thing: ropes; ice axes; crampons; lethal crevasses, rockfall, avalanche . . .'

'I mean . . .'

'But my main interest is travelling. Those are just the games I play when I get there. Yes, travelling is my passion – going on safari, as they say in Kiswahili.'

Aphro sighed. I had moved her – a little further from me, spiritually speaking, if I was any judge. But she remained put physically.

'And so,' I continued, 'I would like to employ someone to look after my flat when I'm away. And when I'm there, of course. I have so little time to pursue my business interests; too busy having fun, you understand. So I would like someone to relieve me of the burden of housework.'

'I don't find the idea of being someone's maid very attractive,' she said simply.

'I don't find the idea of you being someone's maid attractive either,' I replied, with great sympathy.

'Then why are you offering me the job?'

'Max said you needed the money.'

'What business is it of Max's?' she demanded, with mild but sincere outrage. She was very beautiful when angry; mainly, I think, because she still appeared incapable of hurting a fly.

'Oh, he just mentioned it in passing. I think he

thought I should patronize you, because you're such a brilliant student of . . . what is it you're studying?'

'Philosophical Ethics.'

'Ah! A subject very dear to my own heart. If you have just waved a dear friend off from your doorstep, when a man you believe to be a professional assassin – employed to take your friend's life – arrives and asks you which road your friend has taken, should you lie to protect your friend, thus breaking the moral injunction against lying, or should you tell the truth, thus taking the risk of assisting in your friend's murder?'

'Why are you offering me such a ridiculous amount of money?'

I glided effortlessly over her *non sequitur*. 'If a mother is hiding beneath the floorboards with her infant child, together with ten other worthy people, whilst soldiers are searching the building, intent upon executing all twelve of these unjustly persecuted innocents, and if this mother cannot persuade her baby to be silent, should she smother it, thus saving herself and ten others, or should she rather allow her baby to mewl on, thus delivering all twelve into the hands of the enemy?'

'Why won't you answer my question?'

'Why won't you answer mine?'

'Because they're not relevant.'

'Well, what if a man who owns one of the world's great art treasures stipulates in his will that it should be cremated with him when he dies? Should his family respect his wishes? And if they do, should the state then intervene, suspending the laws of property upon which our whole civilization rests . . .'

'I'd say *teeters*, rather than rests,' Aphro interrupted, '. . . or perhaps *sinks*. The laws of property into which our whole civilization sinks.'

Got her!

'You see,' I said, 'these are interesting questions; and they are all interlinked. Should a government use military might to crush an upstart dictator, killing tens or even hundreds of thousands of innocent civilians in the process, and devastating the ecology of a whole region, in order to secure the mineral resources upon which the prosperity of the Western world depends? Did Hamlet have any justification for leaping into Ophelia's grave and entering into a grotesque grieving competition with Laertes, whose loss must have been incomparably greater than his own? Was Medea a good mother?'

'You're raving,' said Aphro – though she was not, I guessed, altogether unimpressed.

I looked at my watch. 'You have to go,' I pointed out.

Aphro looked at her watch. Then she bit her lip.

I shrugged. 'As far as I'm concerned, the job's yours if you want it.'

Aphro stared piercingly at me. 'Are you a pervert?' she asked.

'None of your business,' I lied.

'Are you noisy?' she asked.

'Not particularly,' I said, quite truthfully as it happened.

Aphro looked down at her drink. She seemed depressed.

'I do need more time for my work – I mean my real work,' she admitted.

'Me too,' I concurred.

There was silence: not an unpleasant one, all things considered.

'Then it's settled,' I concluded, holding up my three-quarters-empty glass to her full one. She did not reciprocate my gesture, but looked hard at me again. I did not flinch.* I clearly had her in a corner. John Maynard Keynes did the same thing once with sugar, I believe, or hot air – some commodity or other, I forget which. Buy cheap and sell dear, that's what my dear father always used to say to me, before he was liquidated.

She looked at her watch again. 'I can't decide now,' she said, shaking her head. She reached for her bag. Suddenly, the bar was full of people. 'I'll phone you,' she said.

'Do you have a mobile?' I asked.

She nodded.

---

* Although I did consider vomiting.

I took out my own and brandished it. 'You could ring me now,' I suggested.

She looked exasperated, but not entirely unamused. 'What's your number?'

I gave her all my numbers; she wrote them down in her diary.

'I'm going away soon,' I said.

'I'll ring you before the end of the week,' she said feebly. 'Where is your flat, anyway?'

'Overlooking the Thames, near Waterloo Bridge – about two hundred feet above sea level,' I added wittily.

For the first time since I had met her, a beguiling look of poverty appeared in her eyes. 'And I'd have my own room?'

'And bathroom,' I added. 'Contact would be strictly limited to the communal parts. I mean . . .'

She stood up sharply. Indicating the untouched Virgin Mary, she said, 'Thanks for the drink.'

I gave her a generous smile. We exchanged goodbyes and Cinders left the pub.

It was teeming with humanity.

(why not stay at home?)

So what if life is a bridge, as some old Persian claimed? Why *not* build a home on it? After all, statistical survival rates aren't everything.

I once knew a man whose life was made miserable by mysterious gaps that opened up all around him – between the car he had bought and the car he wanted to drive; between the food he felt like eating when he ordered and the food the waiter then brought him; between the friends he made in his youth and the friends he would prefer to have made; between the women he took to bed and the women he woke up with; between the love his family gave him and the love he felt he needed.*

---

* And I once knew a woman who could only enjoy food if it came from someone else's plate; and yet another man who maintained that the number of sexual partners a man should have at any one time, if

He used to liken his position to that of someone who, knowing exactly what drug he needed to cure him of some nagging ailment, had been let loose in a pharmacy, only to find that the labels had been removed from all the bottles.*

One day I told this friend that I suspected that, at heart, he was a frustrated traveller. The independent traveller, I told him, is for ever discovering gaps – geographical gaps, geological gaps, cartographical gaps; gaps in experience, gaps in knowledge, gaps in space-time – which he or she then proceeds to close. This process, I told him, is known as setting out on a journey.

He must have believed me, for six months later he

---

psychological and emotional health is to be maintained, should be either less than or greater than but in no case equal to one†. Unhappily, after predicting wrongly the likely longevity of a casual fling, his adherence to this theory obliged him to divorce his wife after twenty-three years of happily married life. But that is another story; or, rather, those are two other stories. And since neither of them are travel stories, it is not fitting that they should be included in the present work.

† $(\forall x)(\forall t)Sx \leftrightarrow (p \neq 1)$; where $\forall$ is the universal quantifier, S is sanity, x is a man,‡ and p is the number of sexual partners x, or whatever his name is, has at time t. Conversely $(p = 1) \rightarrow Mx$; where M is madness and x now has only a passing resemblance to a man ($x \approx$ a man).

‡   To be is to be the value of a variable.§

§   To err is human; to move in circles, divine.

*   Perhaps they had been washed off in a flood?

shook the soil from his roots and left England, never to be seen again.

I myself have never suffered from gaps, be they between appearance and reality, expectation and event, imagination and actuality, or the beginning of a sentence and its end, horses. Even so, for those inconsequential discontents that have from time to time beset me, travelling has always been my favourite remedy. For a journey is a tonic that, even when it does not cure the disease outright, will always ameliorate the symptoms. And even when it does not ameliorate the symptoms, it will at least distract the sufferer from his torments. And even when it does not distract the sufferer from his torments, it will, almost certainly, sooner or later come to an end. And if the journey has been an uphill struggle, that may be a blessing in itself.

So it came about that, whenever I began to feel that my life in London was not providing me with that fulfilment which – young, wealthy, healthy, well edu-cated, tolerably good-looking, and indisputably single – I had every right to expect, and even demand, I would solemnly prescribe for myself a trip into the unknown.

(a rare moment of relaxation)

In a pathetic attempt to generate some good karma, I spent the rest of the evening getting drunk and losing large amounts of money to all-comers on the pool table. It's the only way you can guarantee staying on the table all night. The normal rule is winner stays on, but if the loser is sufficiently well heeled, and doesn't object to wearing those heels down by a nanometre or two, the rules can usually be reversed. Not a very good way of generating respect from one's fellow hustler, but what the hell? Even Edmund was beloved.

When I couldn't hit the cue ball any more I staggered out of the pub and directly into the dark, diesel-fired womb of a black cab. Arrived back at the flat as if by magic. Slipped the blind man who lives in the gutter outside my flat a fifty, to reward him for keeping his eyes closed. Experienced sustained difficulties operating the lift, but that's only to be expected with a man of my calibre. Drank five pints of water – in my view the only really effective way of avoiding the unpleasant and wholly unnecessary consequence of enjoying a drink that is known colloquially as a 'hangover' – before sinking into an organic, additive-free slumber (alcohol doesn't count; even elephants get pissed). Sadly, however, this condition only persisted until six o'clock the following morning.

Awoke feeling perky and optimistic.* Made seventeen phone calls to friends' answerphones, just to let them know I was all right, whilst fortifying myself for the day with statesmanlike quantities of Earl Grey tea (with milk). Sat by the phone waiting for someone to return a call.†

I expect you are wondering what I looked like. I was wondering myself, and went to the bathroom specifically in order to find out. I was possibly a little greener than usual, but I was definitely alive, because I could see my eyes moving.

None of this mattered, however, because just before eight o'clock I received a phone call from my new servant, Aphro, who arranged to come and see her place

---

* I.e. largely untroubled by suicidal impulses.

† Sadly, no one was to do so until some twelve hours later. This is not because my friends do not love me, but because they are relatively disadvantaged, and thus obliged to squander their days 'earning' money.

of employment at three o'clock that afternoon. Without bothering about breakfast, I left the flat and took a taxi to my gym, in order to sweat out some of the pleasure which had accumulated in my body over the previous few days.

(fitness for travellers)

For the committed independent traveller – who may have to break out into a trot or even a canter (I will not say pronk) at a moment's notice; or wrestle over their passport with a gang of pre-pubescent pickpockets; or avoid a charging white rhino by stepping deftly behind a handy bush or tree, which those furiously myopic herbivores would never dream of harming – keeping in trim is a serious business. I shall deal later with the vexed question of how to work out in hotels that are not equipped with gyms and swimming pools, detailing exercises that utilize common hotel-room *objets trouvés*, such as empty gin bottles, overhead fans, trouser-presses, mini-refrigerators, mosquito nets, and so on. Here I shall confine myself to a few brief remarks about keeping in trim between trips.

I chose my gym in part because it is open twenty-four hours a day, and I am a poor and irregular sleeper.

For the career insomniac, vigorous exercise in the early hours of the morning has the advantage of relieving one altogether of the tantalizing belief that sleep is still a possibility; once you hit the pain barrier, and the adrenalin is pumping through your arteries hot and fast, you can be absolutely certain you have no chance whatsoever of sleeping until mid-morning. Consequently it becomes far easier to relax and, hopefully, to fall asleep without really intending to.

More importantly, however, I chose my gym for its superb clear-glass façade, which exposes the athletes within to the uncensored gaze of passers-by. Located as it is within the City of London, the stretch of pavement beyond the glass is trodden from early morning until late at night by a plethora of high-status, high-achieving, physically attractive individuals. Many people might feel that no worse arrangement could be imagined, seeing nothing positive whatever in the prospect of humiliating themselves in front of their peers by displaying in public their rippling layers of fat, their sweat-bloated, blood-leeched faces, their scrawn, as they huff and puff and pant and puke gracelessly towards their desired level of exhaustion. After all, what more onanistic, purposeless, absurd expenditure of energy could be imagined? Why would anyone wish to be observed doing such a thing to themselves in public?

That is one view. I, on the other hand, relish the

opportunity to have my own small store of fortitude bolstered by the censorious gaze of passers-by, who have jobs, suits, and homes to go to. Would I spend twenty minutes pulling against some carefully prepared hydraulic resistance on a 'rowing machine'* if I was not being watched? Would you? Then you are a better person than I am.[†]

I try wherever possible to follow the imperative of the Delphic Oracle,[‡] and one of the things I have learned is that I am far more likely to endure the indignity of sweating out that second bottle of Côtes de Bourg with the aid of the panopticon-like architecture of my private gym than I ever would be in private, where there is nothing to stop me from pretending to myself that I never even drank the first.

The budget traveller, whose purse may not stretch to the hundreds or even thousands of pounds a year that a suitably *public* private gym will demand in membership charges, might like to try doing laps around a busy city square or park, possibly whilst dressed from head to toe in pink or yellow Lycra, or maybe whilst clad in the

---

* I was brought up believing that 'machines' were things that did the work for us. One would have expected a half-decent rowing machine to do at least *some* of the rowing. The one I use doesn't even have rollocks; totally impractical for even the most modest sea voyage.
† I expect you had already worked that out.
‡ '*Know thyself*.'

costume of a favourite children's TV character (such as Bramblemousse – see below for details*). I was on the verge of suggesting Leicester Square, but you could hardly expect to stand out from the crowd there without actually dousing yourself with petrol and setting yourself on fire. And, in truth, I can't think of anywhere in London where you might expect to generate the faintest spark of interest in your activities by any means other than violence. But outside the capital, where the customary laws of ridicule still hold sway, fear of being recognized can still inspire above average performances, even when one is feeling jaded.

This technique can easily be adapted to Italian piazzas, French *grandes places*, German *Plätze*, and so on. Indeed, in some more provincial locations, where the archaic sense of community raises the general fear of ridicule to heights undreamed of by modern city dwellers, you may even be fortunate enough to find yourself being harried on your way by a barrage of over-ripe fruit, hurled at you in the authentic pre-Enlightenment spirit of fear, horror and disgust at human otherness.

---

*   Sadly, this chapter was never written.

(final preparations)

After three hours in the sauna, an hour-long massage, half an hour on the sunbed, and five litres of Evian, I was feeling so tanned, fit and healthy that I decided to treat myself to a proper lunch. I succeeded in dragging a friend away from her post, and then in getting her drunk enough to be vaguely amusing. In the spirit of my morning fitness kick, we drank only white wine (sweet Muscat with the foie gras, to replenish the energy I had expended in the gym; Pouilly Fumé to complement the John Dory; more Muscat to wash down pudding; followed with a rather buxom Gewürztraminer, to replace any fluids I may have lost during the course of the meal).

My friend Sandy was in the process of designing a very intelligent disinformation campaign in order to persuade children to eat more sugary snacks. I told her I was about to recruit a live-in domestic. She was very impressed, because she's a shallow, social-climbing snob, who only tolerates my company because I'm so rich. I like her because she flatters me constantly, and because she's one of the few people I know who is without doubt a far worse human being than I am.

Wandered homewards along the Embankment, purchasing armfuls of white lilies and a modest selection of delicacies with which to greet my new employee. Bathed, showered, shaved, cleaned my teeth – three times, with floss – gargled, forgot to spit, pondered over whether or not to call an ambulance, eventually opting to ring a medical friend, who told me he thought I would probably be OK. While I was talking to him I put in an order for some morphine, which is good for pain, which I get a lot. Opened the oysters, set the other dainties on a tray, transferred the vintage Bollinger from the freezer into the refrigerator, and whiled away the next twenty minutes trying to work out how to loll casually on the couch.

(transports of joy)

Aphro rang my bell.

(borderline formalities)

One of the perennial problems faced by the truly independent traveller is how to pass unscathed and, as it
were, unpenetrated through customs and immigration
control. The difficulties one confronts when bicycling
across the border between the Central African Republic
and Zaire, for instance, or Zaire and the Central African
Republic, to take another equal and opposite example,
may well be extreme. More likely than not you will be
confronted by aggressively uncooperative, Kalashnikov-
toting 'government' troops, with little more to offer
them – by way of amends for the justifiable frustration
they feel at having been born ill-mannered, uncouth,
stupid, vindictive, and poor (rather than ill-mannered,
uncouth, stupid, vindictive, and rich, like their privileged
'guests' from Europe and North America) – than the
bell from your bicycle.

Dilemmas abound: if you part with your bell, how

will you alert other road users – trucks, cattle, pedestrians, mule carts, chickens, children, lions, tigers, and bears – to your imminent arrival? Would it not then be preferable to part with your brake blocks? That way, at least, even though you may be approaching at speed, the life forms in your path will be informed of your coming.

When confronting such situations, I recommend that, as far as possible, you should attempt to divest the encounter of its personal dimension. Smile, and cooperate aggressively. If you have had the foresight to bring a teddy, pull the stuffing out of it enthusiastically and fling it willy-nilly, this way and that, across the blood-spattered floor of the piss-drenched customs hovel in which you are about to be raped.

Whatever happens, do not allow the soldiers/guards/customs officers/immigration controllers/genocidal maniacs to see the unalloyed fury and contempt you feel towards them and their vicious, embezzling ways. Try to bear in mind that the development of the iron and steel industry that led ultimately to the production of your bell (though not, as far as I know, to its chromium plating) would never have developed were it not for Britain's barbaric exploitation of the African slave trade. Remember that the continent was depopulated and its economy razed largely for your benefit. Think of your microwave oven, and be glad. But at the same time, try to take a philosophical view of your possessions: You may have selected, bought and paid for your bell; you may have attached it lovingly to the handlebar of your bicycle with a screwdriver and drop-forged, chrome-molybdenum spanner purchased specifically for the purpose; you may have polished and oiled and cleaned it daily, to protect its mechanism from the desert sands – but that does not mean that other people do not have rights over it too. Try to adopt a Taoist, open-handed attitude towards both your luggage and your person, which when all is said and done is just one more material possession.* *All property is theft*† should be your mantra.

Bribery is always worth a try. But remember that, in this type of situation, cheques are seldom accepted and credit cards almost never. Just as the infant bunny rabbit gazes lovingly into the mesmeric eyes of the stoat that is about to devour it, so the US dollar is regarded with awe and reverence throughout the undeveloping world, where it is invariably the preferred unit of currency.

In the most impoverished countries, it can sometimes be difficult to agree on a sensible figure; since there is nothing to buy in the shops, the only sum that could make any appreciable difference to the lives of the despairing, camouflage-clad, machete-wielding murder-

---

* Though not one, it is true, you could easily do without.
† Especially *stolen* property.

ers who so vigorously oppose your holiday plans is the price of one-way tickets to Heathrow for him and his nearest and dearest, with forged UK passports thrown in.

If the fiscal situation does spiral completely out of control, it may be wise to fall back on the bicycle bell stratagem. If resistance continues, try throwing in your brake blocks as well. Do try to keep hold of your bicycle pump, the lack of which can be genuinely crippling; and always keep a supply of fresh condoms at the ready, just in case negotiations go seriously awry. Avoid entering into discussions pertaining to your own or anyone else's religious convictions because, however certain in your own mind you may be that God or Elvis Presley or human rights really do exist, you can be sure that, wherever you may be in the world, at least one person in the room will possess some semblance of rationality, and this can cause disagreements.

A small photograph of somebody's wife and children (your own, if you have any) will sometimes suffice to induce a transitory illusion of fellowship in your tormentors. And, if all else fails, do remember that, despite having fallen into almost complete desuetude in the economically advanced West, begging and pleading can still be effective techniques.

There isn't enough space here to explore in detail a subject that could easily fill an entire volume, but for those of you who have never tried, the general principles of supplication are as follows: your theme should be stated *con brio* but *senza fuoco*; your delivery *mezzoforte*, *lento*, and – ideally – *moderato maestoso*; the development *animato* but the language *sempre semplice*; the approach to the finale should be *stringendo*, but the finale itself *ritardando* and *decrescendo* (this last can be tricky: to many people, jabbering and screaming seem a far more 'natural' way to finish such a performance, especially if the audience happens to be holding a gun to your head at the time). If you're worried about your technique, try improvising in front of a mirror before setting out. Servility and self-abasement should be *riforzando*, and whatever else you do, when their heartstrings are finally *pizzicato*, don't go spoiling everything by attempting a *scherzo*, because you'll probably end up being beaten *con legno*, and possibly even shot.

Possibly of greater interest to the mainstream traveller – who prefers destinations where, in spite of their historic affinity, the sewage and fresh water systems have become permanently estranged and show no immediate likelihood of being reunited – are the problems caused on departure, when passing through airport security; and on arrival, when attempting to clear customs without being finger-fucked by some over-zealous civil servant.

I don't know about you, but whenever anyone in a

uniform so much as looks at me, I can't help assuming I've done something wrong. Why this should be the case is anybody's guess. I suppose that not wearing the same uniform as somebody else is, in strictly human terms, an offence in itself – perhaps it is even the original sin. Dressing up in the uniform of a group which enjoys a strategic alliance with the officials concerned can save a lot of trouble. Impersonating a police officer, however – unless you happen actually to be one – is a criminal offence in Great Britain and Northern Ireland. (Do I hear cries of 'closed shop'?) Traffic wardens have no friends; firemen and nurses seldom travel in uniform; dressing up as an air hostess is, in some respects at least, ideal; but it can lead to surprisingly poor levels of in-flight service. At the end of the day, it's probably best to settle for a suit, tie and briefcase.

When approaching the discourteous, odiferous, nylon-clad knicker-sniffers who staff security barriers around the globe, do remember that they are only trying to do their job. Take good care neither to catch, nor to avoid catching, anybody's eye. Don't bother emptying your pockets before walking through the metal detector, because they're all tuned to different sensitivities depending on whether or not the security staff enjoy feeling up the passengers. If you're up against a consortium of erotomaniacs, the machine will scream blue murder at the fillings in your teeth; if you're dealing with a cube of frigid types, you can carry through a .38 handgun and five clips of live ammunition without raising a peep.

If you do get frisked, try to enjoy it; after all, it's not often you can get that sort of treatment for nothing. But if you're really not enjoying yourself, and you suspect the same-sex security officer of heterosexuality, try swivelling your hips and groaning. If you suspect they're gay, maintain an erect posture. If you suspect you're gay, approach the security zone as a 'safe space' for experimentation; fly frequently and carry as much loose change as you can fit in your pockets. Snappy dressers may console themselves by reflecting that the goon concerned is unintentionally smoothing the creases from your jacket and trousers. And if you are unfortunate enough to have metal in your body, as I have where my heart used to be, then you will, like me, be grateful for all the attention you can get.*

Clearing customs can be an altogether more difficult matter. The main options are going for Green and keeping your fingers crossed, or going for Red and

---

* Though not homosexual myself (what could a man possibly have to offer me that I don't possess at least one of myself?) I am not so prejudiced against my own sex as to feel wholly indifferent to having some warm-fingered, sweaty young stallion describing my surface contours with deft, reassuring movements of his hands. Physical contact with another human being can be a great emollient, just so long as it stops short of a punch.

keeping your fingers crossed. In either case your luggage may well be unpacked, giggled over, and paraded before the eager eyes of your fellow passengers. For this reason, I strongly advise keeping soiled underwear and sex toys wrapped in brown paper bags; few if any customs officers will feel inclined to thrust their hand in and rummage around, and neither are they very likely to empty the contents out, for fear you should insist that they repack these items themselves. If a kilo of coke or an illicitly extracted human body part *has* somehow found its way into your luggage, basically you're fucked. And do remember, strange as it may seem, erect penises are still illegal in Great Britain and Northern Ireland.

(departure date)

'Do you like seafood? You'll find the beluga goes particularly well with the Bollinger. The words sound rather nice together too, don't you think? Beluga ... Bollinger ... be-lollinger ... be-lollinger-gallula ... be-lu-la-lol-in-gallula ...'

'You are mad!'

'Sorry?'

'Max told me that I shouldn't take anything you do or say seriously, because you're completely mad.'

'Sweet of him. Have an oyster. I must warn you, that sauce is a little peppery. It goes very nicely with the oyster itself, but you may find yourself less able to appreciate the other little morsels I've laid on.'

'I'll stick to lemon, thank you. Mmm ... wow, that's fantastic.'

'Let me top you up.'

'Um, thank you. I've got to go at four.'

'Labouring?'

'Tutorial.'

'Good. Glad to see you're getting down to it, in spite of everything.'

'What everything?'

'Changing jobs; moving homes . . . very stressful time in a person's life. Rates second only to . . . I forget what . . . holidays? . . . divorce? . . . sex? . . . death? . . . something like that. Moving homes comes second to something else in the stress tables.'

'Do you suffer a lot of stress, Otto?'

'Why do you ask?'

'The way you're sitting. You look rather . . . rigid.'

'No, no. I worked out and had a massage today, that's all. I'm probably sitting awkwardly because I'm feeling so – you know – extremely *well*.'

'Ah, I see.'

'Do lie down on the le Corbusier if you feel like stretching out.'

'Thank you, I'm fine.'

'Yes, you look fine.'

A silence ensued, broken only by the faint sound of munching.

'Mm . . .'

'So you accept my offer then?'

'What? What did you say?'

'It's all right, calm down. I was asking you if you accept my offer of a job.'

'I'm trying to think about it.'

'Crevette?'

'Um . . . yes, thank you. Are you not having any?'

'I ate earlier.'

'Oh, I see. Gosh.'

Another silence; this time without munching.

'I can see there's something on your mind. You have some reservations?'

'Why are you doing this? I mean, are you just trying to seduce me? You could go about it a lot more cheaply than this, you know. I'm not promising you'd succeed, but . . . what's going on?'

'Going on? Nothing, nothing whatsoever. No, my intentions are completely . . . what's the word . . . oh, what is that word?'

'Obscure?'

'Venerable . . . no, that's not it.'

'Honourable?'

'Honourable, that's the one. Hadn't heard it for such a long time I'd almost forgotten how to pronounce it. Yes, my intentions are completely honourable. I want someone to perform little tasks around the house; you need money; Max likes you – so I just put two and two together and . . . Hey presto!'

'Do you have a criminal record?'

'Not as far as I know. You never can tell, of course, but no, I don't suppose so. There have been parking tickets, of course. Why, do you?'

'No.'

'So what's your interest?'

'I'm trying to work out if you're dangerous.'

'Oh, no. No, I shouldn't think so. No. I'm a bit unsteady on my feet at times, but that doesn't generally create a hazard for other people. No, you've nothing to worry about where that's concerned. I'd actually go as far as to say I'm an exceptionally harmless person. Like in that song by Purcell, "Only the Harmless and the Good". You know – from *The Faerie Queen*?'

'I don't know it.'

'I won't sing it for you; I might take away your appetite.'

Laughter.

'Anyway, in the song, only the harmless and the good are allowed to do something. I forget what. Anyway, whatever it is, I'm harmless, so I'm allowed to.'

'I see. You accord yourself special privileges?'

'I'm stinking rich, you mean?'

'No, I meant moral privileges.'

'Oh no, I don't have any of those. I've no right to anything. If you ask me, no one has. But that's just a personal opinion: you can have all the rights you want. But yes, I am stinking rich. Absolutely reeking.'

'Max told me that you've been ruined by your money – that if you hadn't had any, or just a normal amount, you could have done something with your life.'

'You and Max talk a lot, do you?'

'A bit. He described you as a poor imitation of an adult cobbled together by a teenage boy from the debris he found at the scene of a disaster.'

Another silence – this one mine, as it happens.

'What was the disaster?' Aphro asked gently.

'You know that he fancies you?' I squealed. 'He admitted it to me on the phone.'

'Oh . . . Yes, I suppose I did know that.'

'Yes, watch him. He's a man of unusual tastes.'

'Otto!'

'I'm not saying another word. You've been warned.'

'That's slanderous!'

'Not if it's true, it's not.'

'And is it?'

'Haven't a clue. Probably . . . How would I know? Let me top you . . . Here.'

'Thank you. You're getting me drunk.'

'Good. I mean, that's what champagne is for, really, isn't it. I'm a firm believer in Aristotelian teleology. The material cause of champagne is the grape; its effective cause is fermentation; its formal cause is the *méthode champagnoise*; and its final cause is to get ordinary people like you and me pissed on a Tuesday afternoon.'

'You're clever, aren't you? I mean – intelligent?'

'No, not at all. What makes you say that?'

'Something you said.'

'You must have misheard me.'

'Can I see the bedroom?'

'Whose bedroom? I mean, I live on my own here, so they're both my bedrooms, so that's not a meaningful question. Actually, I should say all three of them are mine, but I use one of them as a study. You mean the room that is yours for the asking?'

'I suppose that's what I mean, yes.'

'It's that door over there. It's en suite.'

Aphro tottered over to explore her new quarters. She returned three minutes later.

'It's fantastic. I can't believe the view. You've got such a great flat.'

'So you'll stay?'

'What, now? No.'

'I'm leaving for Frankfurt on Friday.'

'Frankfurt? What are you going to do in Frankfurt?'

'I haven't decided yet. But it's an important trip.'

'I see. Five hours' work a week?'

'More or less – probably less. All expenses paid; salary

by direct debit into your bank account. Or, if you preferred, I could pay you in camels.'

'I don't smoke.'

'Good joke. I liked that. Yes, good one.'

'But you didn't laugh.'

'I don't. It's just not one of my things. Never really liked ball games either.'

'My God, you are strange.'

'Are you a believer?'

'Pardon?'

'In the being whose name you just invoked.'

'No, just loose talk. Why, are you?'

'No, it just made me wonder – when you mentioned him. Because he can't hear you, you know, when you talk to him. I mean, I wouldn't know, I've never tried. But he doesn't exist, does he? *Ergo* he can't hear you. No one can hear you . . . We're all alone. I mean, there are two of us here . . . but we're still alone.'

'That's what I'm worried about.'

'I'm sorry, I didn't mean to suggest . . .'

'I was joking. Don't worry. You seem OK. Max says you're safe – safe as a fruit-bat, he said.'

'Nice of him. You'll do it, then?'

'How about a trial period, to see how we get on?'

My heart beat. 'Fine,' I shrugged indifferently.

'But . . .'

'What?'

'. . . you can't give me all that money. It's ludicrous. It makes me feel . . . Oh, God, look at the time, I've got to go. Look, I'll ring you.'

She left.

My flat was absolutely huge.

(to Hackney, to take the air)

My usual purveyor of mood-altering substances – a charming, well-connected Eton-educated man by the name of Trog – had recently been unusually difficult to track down. And so, feeling in need of an excursion, the very next day I decided to take a trip to Hackney, to see if I could pick up a few staples to tide me over.

I had heard that in a particular area of Hackney it was possible to buy drugs from the police (as they are laughingly known by the locals); but unfortunately that service had recently been discontinued, driven into abeyance by the forces of reaction, who maintain that the public and private sectors should retain their historic separation on these shores.

I dressed down (Versace jeans and T-shirt, Nike trainers, black USAF fighter-pilot jacket), jumped on the tube, and only forty-five minutes later found myself wandering amongst the bosky woods, crystalline rills, and verdant pastures of Dalston. The litter-strewn tarmac of Kingsland High Street was creaking beneath the weight of traffic – stomping northwards, stomping southwards, going nowhere. No blueberries, even in the shops; perhaps I was in the wrong part of Hackney. But the sky was still there, high up in the sky, shying away, receding from view. It is the same everywhere in this city. I expect if you looked at it from the side you would see that the sky over London has a bulge in it, as a shroud bulges over a corpse. At certain points the shroud and corpse make contact, as on Hampstead Heath, for instance, which I suppose must be the nose, or the forehead, or possibly the penis. At other points the shroud hangs far above the flesh – at the neck, for instance, or the navel. In between is dead space.

Dalston is perhaps the nook between the thighs. The celestial drapery is a long way off here. The human spirit did not die here, though; no, fleeing from tourists in the West End, it got lost at Highbury Corner, expended its last drops of energy on the Blackhorse Road, and keeled over once and for all by the railway station at Finsbury Park. When the weather is hot, I believe you can just about detect the odour of rotting immortality as you walk up the Seven Sisters Road.*

---

* I say 'you' and I mean 'you'; I would be in a taxi, with the windows wound tightly up.

Ridley Road market was bustling with bargain hunters: cheerful Africans, morose Englanders, and the occasional mysterious, land-lorn Kurd. In a shopping mood myself, I wandered down Dalston Lane, looking out for significant loiterers. Around an hour later I happen upon a scrofula of feral teenagers (a 'posse') who seem interested in me. Judging from their complexions, I am encouraged in my belief that they will be able to tell me where best to do my shopping. It turns out I am correct in my assumption.

Two of them lead me to a nearby block of flats and into the urinous lift. If I am going to be mugged, I realize, it will happen here. But these children are not interested in mugging me; indeed, they have taken a liking to me, for I look fairly cool to them, and treat them as equals. They, like me, do not know the meaning of poverty: they because they have worn its uniform and born its trappings for such a long time that, like well-trained soldiers, they do not notice the burden they carry; I because I have never experienced it. They are intelligent, witty, foul-mouthed, almost wholly uneducated, and full of fascination and respect for physical violence. But basically they are hurt and sad and frightened, and I get along with them fine, for I am small for my height, and would even go so far as to say that the only person I have ever scared is myself. They have dead eyes and are confused by politeness, though they enjoy the attention I pay them. Even so, I attempt to restrain my natural courtesy a little, in case they should remark, in my polished behaviour, a reflection of their own uncouth and clouded souls, and take this revelation as an insult. Even the least refined among us, if we are honest, is not so coarse-grained that he can remain indifferent to the image of his own churlishness.

Having given a rough outline of my requirements in the lift, I was abandoned on the twenty-first floor and invited to enjoy the view to the west, whilst my new friends contacted the small businessmale or small businessfemale (it turned out to be a businessmale) they intended to introduce me to. Off they scampered up the stairs. My heart was pounding rather heavily, I must admit, as I stood there in the corridor. Stale cooking smells, obscene graffiti, broken bits of building, the smell of rotting vermin: the disgust I felt towards this environment screamed murder at me – my murder, the boys' murder, anybody's murder. For something needed revenging. My clothes felt terribly clean – crisp, almost – and luxurious; and my skin seemed to me suddenly very soft and delicately scented (it is). I felt vaguely sacrificial. Did they hate me? I wondered. Did I them? Did we each other?

A wrinkled old West Indian man appeared from one of the flats and walked towards me, humming to himself. I flinched as he approached, grasping my roll of notes, preparing to thrust it manfully into his hands should he so much as bid me good morning. He smiled and touched his forehead as he passed, as if he had once worn a cap there, and was still addicted to displays of deference. I felt embarrassed, and considered giving him the money anyway, out of . . . well, certainly not out of generosity. But the boys returned before my guilty impulse could bear fruit. They told me I had to wait.

We stared out of the window together, the two youngsters spitting on the floor, turn and turn about, to show their disrespect for the inhabitants of this tower, and for floors generally. One of them gobbed on the ceiling. Then, for the sake of completeness, the other gobbed on the wall. Our conversation was running dry. I wondered vaguely if the sky was forced upwards everywhere they put up high-rise buildings. I tried to remember how close to the ground the sky was in New York.

A tall, leering, head-fucked white man – somewhere between twelve and sixty years of age – wandered past us, grimacing and sneering and looking like he wanted to kill something, or someone; or like he just had – a rat, perhaps, or a dog – and very much wanted to do it again. The two boys pretended they did not know him, dissembling crudely. Then they left me again.

Compared with meeting Trog at some pleasant bar in Kensington, this seemed like a rigmarole. Still, Trog wasn't available; and when one's usual supply of home comforts runs out, one is inevitably forced to venture abroad. People seldom stab you, just so long as you do not attempt to thwart their will in any way. It is when others make resistance to their plans that people do not like it – although outright capitulation can enrage people too. A friend of mine had his teeth pulled out at a cashpoint machine, with nothing but a kick in the head for anaesthetic. That, the police told him, was because he had been too cooperative. You have to let them see the pain and humiliation they are causing you, he was told, otherwise they will grow frustrated and cause you some more.

When I am mugged I always try to split the money fifty-fifty with the mugger. It seldom works, in the sense that few muggers are idiot enough not to realize that they hold all the cards, and can beat you down relentlessly; but it does help the inadequate, thieving little shit who is holding a craft-knife to your gut to retain a little pride during the transaction, for he feels that he has been to work, throwing his weight about like a proper businessmale, and in consequence is less likely to use the implement concerned to carve his initials on your forehead. Fighting back is always worth considering, but only try this if you actually like hurting people; as with most things, if you don't enjoy it you're unlikely to be any good at it. By throwing a half-hearted punch, then standing still while people hit, kick and stab you back, you may be guilty of sending out mixed messages. Like-wise, running away should only be attempted by those who are blessed with a genuine streak of cowardice.

The boys returned, led me back into the lift, up one floor, and along the corridor. They were beginning to bristle with excitement, which I found rather chilling, for their attitudes suggested that something was about to happen, and that it was about to happen to me. But I think they were just excited for me, for I was going shopping, and for themselves, for I had promised them a tip.

They took me to the entrance of one of the flats. The door was reinforced with a steel outer-shell, perhaps by the local authority, in order to help people to store their drugs more securely, I suppose. I knocked. The door opened and I went in. As I entered the room a figure was just disappearing through another door.

The room itself seemed haunted by the wraith of departed pleasure. The carpet was a most nauseating electrified orange colour, tangerine, perhaps, or kumquat. There was nothing else in the room except a few pieces of broken-down furniture, scores of empty beer cans, and thousands of spliff-stubs. Something had failed here, failed without even having tried – failed even to try.

I walked over to the window and once again looked out over the city. It stank of tobacco smoke and faeces and dampness; but perhaps that was the flat. Despite the filth, the carpet was rather dazzling, and consequently the city looked very gray, like miscellaneous parings of tarnished pewter on some old-fashioned workshop floor. I stepped out on to the balcony. Even from up here the blue seemed diffident, as if the city had just done something obscene and the sky was pretending not to notice. The clouds looked dirty, like cotton wool that had been used to degrease the city's pores.

I heard the sound of breaking glass, somewhere far away. A car crash? Then it came again. I looked down. In the car park below, the real work of the city was going on: a middle-aged woman was smashing the windows of a car. It seems she had loaded one of her shopping bags with a half brick. Working methodically, but swinging the bag with real panache, she took out the front and rear windscreens, all four side windows, and the driver's side quarterlight. I think her arm had grown fatigued by the time she reached the nearside quarterlight, for she failed three times to smash it. She did not linger to complete her work; it would seem her sense of justice was approximate and that, roughly speaking, justice had been done. Aristotle would have approved.

This interlude did nothing to calm my nerves. I was growing increasingly alarmed by my predicament; so alarmed, in fact, that I rather felt like punching myself in the face – so as to get it over with, and so as to make it clear, when the time came, that I already understood the point that my attackers were trying to make. I re-entered the room. To my left was the doorway through which the figure had disappeared as I entered. A movement caught my attention; it was the leery, head-fucked man.

'What do you want?' he asked.

'Peace on earth; the cancellation of third-world debt, coupled with political policies directed at producing genuinely sustainable development; a state education system that the whole country can be proud of; five grams of coke; five grams of speed; and a family-sized bag of grass, please.'

He looked at me as if the first part of my message had disgusted him, but was willing to quell his burgeoning dislike when he heard the second part, which had inspired him with great enthusiasm. We discussed the price. He gave me a money-back guarantee on quality, and I came as close to laughing as I ever have in my life. We settled on a round figure. I declined his generous offer to look after my cash – recklessly disregarding his warning that we were in a very rough area where muggings were commonplace – and he disappeared again. I counted out the consideration.

The man reappeared less than two minutes later. He

had with him a small boy, six years old at most, who moved about the room in nervous bounds, like a little white-faced monkey. From a distance the boy showed me the drugs. The quantities looked about right. The man stood by the door and counted my money. When he was given the nod, the boy handed the drugs over to me. Man and boy then disappeared as one, without a word, and I followed them as quickly as I could. By the time I had emerged into the corridor they had gone.

The two boys, my contacts, picked me up at the entrance to the building. They nagged and nagged for drugs, but I would not give them any, for they were only young. I gave them cash instead, explaining that they would certainly get a better deal than I did, and that it made no sense to be paid in kind when the cash would go further. I finally made them understand the economic logic, and they were delighted by the generosity of my tip. I had enjoyed their company and, having tasted the white stuff in the lift, which didn't seem at all bad, I felt no compunction in giving them their due.

On the westbound train between Dalston Kingsland and Highbury & Islington the old man sitting next to me died. It only took one stop for him to pass away. I know he was alive when I sat down, for he very kindly moved his knees in order to let me reach the window seat. But when I stood up again and brushed past him in order to disembark, he fell off his seat and slumped to the floor. Blood was flowing out of his ears. I pulled the emergency cord and phoned for an ambulance.

Uncharacteristically, I did not wait for the emergency services to arrive, but sidled away, my indulgences – which I carried in my inside breast pocket – pressing hard against my pounding heart.

(base camp)

Aphro came round with all her stuff.

'I didn't know it would be you,' I said to her as I let her in.

'It's not,' she answered, dryly.

'Not who?' I asked, perplexed.

'Whoever you think it is.'

It was mid-afternoon. I went out to do the shopping, while Aphro settled into her room and did some studying. For the evening I was planning a simple collation of goat's-cheese *crostini* with fresh cranberries, followed by *gnocchi* with a *pesto* sauce.*

Fortunately, after spending most of the day searching for something to amuse Aphro with – the importance of

---

*   I grow the basil myself; a good hard *pecorino* is all I needed. Cut the basil at the last moment, to avoid the bitter chemicals released by the plant when under attack.

keeping one's employees in spirits cannot be overstressed – over dinner I finally discovered a topic which proved a source of endless fascination to her: the carryings on of the couple who shared the flat downstairs, who were at that time attempting to sell up in order to pay for their divorce. The way they were going about it, anyone would think their marriage vows had meant something to them.

Their legal expenses were already so great that, had the wife accepted the original settlement without demur, they would both have been better off. Still, they were determined to fight the case all the way, so as to get the correct 'answer'. Their case had already been twice before the House of Lords. I expect they had a flamboyant wedding, too.

Their determination to be violently separated was extraordinary; it united them in opposition to the best advice of friends and lawyers. My view was that they would be back together again soon, once they had worked off their frustrations. At least, I couldn't imagine anyone else wanting them, since they had shown themselves so full of venom.

Aphro looked upon this scenario, which I expounded to her in considerable detail, as she might a cage of scrapping lions – as impressed by the vigour of the warring parties as she was disturbed by the unnecessary cruelty of their conflict. This brought it home to me how much younger Aphro was than myself, because I only found the couple amusing.

I didn't feel at all sleepy after we had eaten. But Aphro did, and went straight to bed, while I tackled the washing up and then settled down with a book.

The following morning, I had just put down the novel I was reading and – having run out of amphetamine-sulphate powder some hours earlier – was considering whether to pop 10 mg Temazepam and call it a day (so to speak), when Aphro emerged unexpectedly from her room. I happened to be seated directly opposite her door at the time. There was nothing untoward in this; I like to range freely around my flat whilst reading; seeking out that exact combination of a certain quality of light, together with the precise physical arrangement of my limbs and torso, that will propitiate a full and vigorous engagement with the work in question. On this particular evening I had finally settled on an antique Italian chair of the kind that is constructed from two sets of interlocking, s-shaped struts joined together at the centre of the seat, a bizarre yet eminently practical combination of papal throne and deckchair. I was illuminated by halogen.

I will not tell you the title of my book, because that would only scare you. But it was fully absorbing my attention. On the table beside me, naturally enough, were a small mirror, a few scraps of Clingfilm, an antique, ivory-handled cut-throat razor, and a pot of Tipp-Ex.

I may have looked a little drawn, I don't know, but when Aphro emerged from her room to find me sitting directly opposite her door she leaped right out of her skin. I did too, as I had forgotten that she was in there. That's why I was there, camping outside her door: sheer forgetfulness had driven me to it. There were more than enough other places for me to sit in my flat – which is, quite frankly, absurdly large, and if anything slightly overfurnished – had I but remembered the pressing need to do so.

'I'm sorry!' I shrieked at her – an admission of guilt which made me look more blameworthy than I perhaps was.

'You made me jump,' she said.

She was wearing pyjamas.

'I was reading. Sorry, I wasn't expecting you to be up so early.'

'Is it so early?' she asked, blurry-eyed.

I looked at my watch. 'It's . . . ten,' I say. I look again: 'Ten-ish; I can't see properly. I was up reading all night.'

I pick up my belongings and wander off towards the other end of the flat, leaving her to ponder my strange behaviour at her leisure. She doesn't seem unduly concerned; probably she is still overwhelmed by the perfect comfort, warmth and silence of her new accommodation.

I take my downers and make myself a breakfast of eggs. I go into my bedroom (54 square metres) to eat it, not wanting to get in Aphro's way. I lurk in my room until I hear her leave the flat, then return to the kitchen, still not feeling remotely tired. Is it the speed, or are the ... responsibilities of an employer causing this unwonted ante-meridian perkiness? I ask myself. It is now eleven o'clock. Something strikes me about the kitchen. I look around, trying to work out what it is. Suddenly I grasp it: Aphro has done the washing up. Joy leaps in my blood like a salmon swimming upriver.* I run my finger over the work surface where my egg shells had lain, bleeding their albumen: it is perfectly clean and dry. Her work was perfect. Tears spring to my eyes. I return to my room, yawning contentedly.

I'm so pleased I do not sleep until gone noon.

---

* Shortly before being netted, smoked and vacuum-packed.

(travel writing)

Now that Aphro is safely out of the flat and you can have no immediate cause to worry, I will tell you which book I was reading. It was *American Psycho* by Brett Easton Ellis. *American Psycho* is a brilliant book, all about a man who goes around New York killing people. In some respects a traditional piece of travel writing, albeit focusing on shorter journeys, mainly by taxi, the book is in other respects highly unconventional, not least in that, in my edition, it sports a photograph on the back cover not of the author himself, but of his fictional counterpart, the mass-murderer Bateman.

This book made a considerable impression on my first reading, giving me both nightmares and panic attacks for a good* fortnight after I had finished reading it. Great literature should have an effect on your life; art

---

* I use the word strictly in its quantitative signification.

should never be merely anodyne. That is why I follow Franz Kafka in making it a rule only to read books that bite and sting me.

Of course, one can adopt many different reading strategies when approaching a challenging work such as this diary of a flesh-eating merchant banker, or whatever he is. My chosen strategy involved a bottle of Tipp-Ex, which I used to obliterate all the passages involving acts of violence. The admirably penned pornography; the hilariously vicious dinner-table banter; the brilliant jokes about social conformity and personal uniformity in that (supposedly) most 'individualistic' of all nations; the brilliantly evoked sense of fatigue at the relentless categorical imperative earned wealth brings in its wake (*enjoy!*); and the heart-wrenching moments of self-revelation, when traveller Bateman betrays just how scared and lonely and hypersensitive to human cruelty he really is: all this I leave unexpurgated.

Why did I do this?

Was I offended? Was I scared? Was I making self-indulgent, sentimental, pseudo-moralistic judgements regarding work that should properly be judged in accordance with purely aesthetic criteria?

No, yes, no, at least I don't think so.

Mainly, I just didn't believe those passages; I simply didn't believe they were *true*. I felt that Easton Ellis had *made them up*. I thought he was *lying* about all that violence. I couldn't see how someone capable of enjoying sexual intercourse with his fellow human beings as much as Bateman does could go on to perform such appalling acts of cruelty and violence. I simply cannot believe that people have such extremes in them – cannot believe that someone can first be very nice to someone and then very, very nasty immediately afterwards, for no clear reason. Maybe I'm being naïve. I mean, I realize that I'm a pretty straightforward kind of guy, and that I don't have the stress of a City career or anything like that to deal with. But – excuse me? – walking around a room with a woman's freshly decapitated head spiked on your erect penis? Hello?

And so I obliterated the offending passages. Then I painted over the word 'Psycho' on the front cover, leaving the title reading *American* (which I thought pretty snappy, actually). Then I cut a photograph of Brett Easton Ellis from the cover of another of his books and sellotaped it over the picture of Bateman.

Then I sat down and read the book again.

This time, I thoroughly enjoyed it. In fact, I read it cover to cover in one sitting. Poor Bateman: so unhappy, so fragile, so vulnerable. The bit where he admits he has no need to work, and that he does so only because he wants to be 'normal' is deeply moving.

My next project would be *Great Expectations*, from which I would extirpate all reference to Estella's mistreatment at the hands of the beastly Bentley Drummle, which I thought almost entirely spoiled the happy ending.*

I was spewed out of dreamland in a cold sweat at around 3.30 p.m. Aphro was crashing around in the kitchen, making herself something to eat. My body was slick with what felt like bile, my mouth dry as the Limpopo in January, and I was suffering from an overwhelming sense of foreboding, as though Death had been hiding under my bed all afternoon and the rotten stench of his breath had penetrated my skin.

Amazed by the amount of noise Aphro was making, I began to wonder whether I should consider renting or possibly even purchasing a separate flat, where I could go in order to sleep undisturbed. I could make an offer to Mr and Mrs Punchandjudy. Their flat isn't as nice as mine, but it would be worthwhile having it available so as to secure myself a decent night's sleep now and then. My head was aching, my jaws were aching (from grinding my teeth together in my sleep), and I felt I had gained no benefit whatsoever from having been unconscious for the previous three hours.

As you might have guessed, I don't really like being

---

* For which the dewy-eyed Bulwer-Lytton fought so valiantly against the drearily pessimistic Dickens.

unconscious. For one thing, waking up always comes as such a shock, and if there's one thing I hate,* it's a surprise. But I also find the whole experience a little vertiginous; I mean, consciousness is suspended over an abyss, is it not? And supposing you do eventually emerge from the somnolent state, how can you be sure that you will wake up the same person you were when you fell asleep? If, like me, you have put a great deal of effort into making sure that your personality is reasonably socially *viable*, if you know what I mean, then this can pose a real threat.

Sleeping is a kind of baptism, only you never know until you actually climb into the font whether you're going to be blessed or boiled – at which point it's too late to do anything about it. Yet the outcome can have a very real impact on the sort of person you are going to be that day – maybe even for the rest of your life.

It's not only the personality-warping dreams that put me off sleep, though; it's also that feeling I get, which I imagine is probably pretty common amongst men of my age (we just don't like to talk about it, right?), that more likely than not I will wake up in the middle of the night to find a madman poised over me with an axe, or a meat cleaver, or a baseball bat, or I don't know what,

---

* Actually, there's more than one.

but something they're intending to use to inflict harm upon me, in interesting and inventive ways. Not that I'm frightened of being mutilated and/or murdered in my bed; I just don't like the idea of waking up to it out of the blue.

So, even though I hadn't slept more than five hours in the last forty-eight (the previous night I had spent with my good friend Tiss, dissolving my *septum nasi* in cocaine), I actually wasn't *that* upset that Aphro had woken me. I was still alive and, so far as I could tell, I hadn't turned into Bateman. So, as naps go, the outcome was largely favourable. And it was mid-afternoon, so Aphro could be forgiven for assuming that I was either out of the house, or working.

I put on my dressing gown and staggered into the kitchen, hunching over my pain as though it was a flame I was warming myself by. Aphro did not hear my bare feet padding across the slate tiles.

'Morning,' I said.

'Oh, hello,' said Aphro. 'Do you want some coffee?' She was wearing a pullover and jeans and tennis pumps, and looked both absolutely radiant and absolutely normal.

'Thanks.'

'Have you eaten?' she asked me casually.

I shook my head.

'I was doing some cheese on toast.'

'Sounds good,' I said vaguely.

I opened the blinds. This was a mistake, for the sunlight screeched like piccolos and snare drums, abrading my retinas.* I flinched as my eyelids battled valiantly against the glare, but they were too thin to hold it back. Even so, I could not bring myself to lower the blind again, because that would involve admitting what a state I was in. So I stood there until the colour came back into the room and the soreness subsided from my eyes and head. And, painful though it was, the bright sunlight had the distinct advantage of picking out the bronze in Aphro's hair.

'Well,' I said at last, 'it's a beautiful day.'

Aphro smiled. She seemed preoccupied.

I harassed her for a response. 'Had a good day? An interesting lecture?'

'So-so,' she said, smiling. 'I've got to write an essay this evening. I'm trying to sort it out in my head.'

'Oh, well, if you want anyone to discuss it with . . .' I offered.

'Thanks,' she said indifferently.

I felt underdressed, and it struck me that my pyjamas and dressing gown, which were silk, might have been making Aphro feel awkward, for she didn't seem to want to look at me, never mind talk. I returned to my room

---

* A nasty case of synaesthesia.

and dressed. But when I got back Aphro paid no more attention to me than she had before. She gave me my coffee, together with what had turned, with neither discussion nor consultation of any kind, into a full-blown *croque monsieur*, using the last of the béchamel sauce I made earlier in the week. Then she left me on my own. This was fine with me, because *croque monsieur* is my favourite breakfast dish. Even so, it didn't bode well for our working relationship, since one would rather expect one's views would be solicited, or at the very least that one would be informed in good time, when a change of menu was to be effected.

Perhaps Aphro is distracted by her work, I reasoned with myself; people with Aphro's intelligence can often be a little bit scatty. Then I noticed that she had left the cooking things unwashed – had not, in fact, so much as placed the dirty plates in the dishwasher. I began to wonder whether I should hire someone to clean up after her.

In the end, after vacillating for around half an hour, wandering in and out of the kitchen, staring wildly at the bread knife, the breadboard, the bowl that had contained the béchamel, the cafetière, and the plates on which Aphro had laid out the ham and cheese slices before transferring them to the bread, I began to wonder at my strange behaviour and got on with the washing up myself.

This left me feeling so relieved – so pure of heart – that I felt sufficiently energized to tackle a rather dull-looking book about managing your own investments that had arrived through the post earlier that morning.

(the price of genius)

Independent travel, in the modern sense of the word –
which I take it most people would agree excludes traipsing across continents, slavishly following herds of ante-
lope as they migrate towards pastures new – would not
be possible were it not for the convenience of money.
Before the idea of a universal portable commodity –
something which can be exchanged for anything, and
anything exchanged for it – had evolved, if you wanted
to go further than a day or two from your homestead it
was necessary to take cattle and grain and other goods
along with you, to barter and to live off during your
journey.

So it is that, if they intend to roam very far from
home, it is imperative that any truly independent traveller knows at least a little about the nature of the
moneybeast. In particular, they should know how to
make it breed.

I learned the basics somewhat late in life, from Henri Fox-Farrier's classic work, *Square Mile of Smiles*. But before I go into the details of the investment strategy I created with the help of that book, I think it is worthwhile mentioning that if, believing as I believe that human nature changes little from epoch to epoch, you have ever found yourself asking where our deeper spirituality can have secreted itself in this seemingly most cynical of ages, I am now in a position to give you the satisfaction you crave: it has resurfaced in the guise of the investment self-help manual.

The distinguishing characteristics of the genre are a self-consciously uplifting prose-style; an emphatic denunciation of the (blasphemous) actions, attitudes and beliefs that will lead ultimately to an investor's downfall and damnation; an equally emphatic but this time more lyrical eulogizing of the (pious) actions, attitudes and beliefs that will lead to an investor's salvation; strong emphasis on the 'fact' that the way of truth is so simple that, while a child could easily manage it, adults tend to find the way hard, for they are wilful, fearful and purblind; a certain amount of more or less scholarly disputation regarding the nature of grace and predestination; lengthy discussions of the importance of faith, patience and discipline in any investor's life, whatever 'strategy' they may adopt for expressing their profound love of money; and, finally, a heartening, almost evangelical enthusiasm for sharing the tips and rules of thumb that brought the author riches (or so they would have us believe) and, therefore, must surely suffice to bring any other devoted acolyte of Mammon into the same lofty spiritual condition.

Which makes me wonder whether the dialectical progress of Western culture has reached its end point not in the revolutionary realization of a communistic utopia, as Marx predicted, but rather in a more straightforward materialist inversion: Heaven is an early and well-funded retirement. The earthly trials that went before will pale into insignificance, so balmy will those final years of placidity, gentle pleasure, and gradual physical dissolution prove. As Christ was for centuries throughout Europe, so money is now the portal by means of which we humble creatures aspire to enter heaven.

I myself have always wanted my pleasure here and now, on the spot, immediately, thank you very much. Indeed, ten minutes' delay is often more than I can bear. This creates problems in itself, of course. The pleasure of the male orgasm, for instance, lasts on average for fifteen or twenty seconds; the ejaculation itself for perhaps five. This pleasure is more intense than the pleasure that precedes it, and far, far preferable to the state of discomfort and exhaustion that follows.

Now, if one devotes all one's energy to the task, in

my experience it is possible to copulate perhaps six or seven times a day. Taking the higher figure of twenty seconds for the whole climactic caboodle, and the less stressful figure of six for the maximum sustainable number of ruttings per day, a quick calculation shows that fucking can, at best, bring only two minutes of really intense pleasure in twenty-four hours, a mere thirty seconds of which could not conceivably be bettered. This means that approximately one seven hundred and twentieth (0.0014) of your day is spent in the state to which you aspire, a mere 0.00035 being what you might call really *heavenly*. The rest of one's time is spent alternately aspiring and recovering.

The mathematics looks bad, I grant you. But the reality need not be quite so grim: in between ruttings you can amuse yourself with conversation, food, television, and drugs. Even so, the quantitative, Benthamite, approach to pleasure would appear to suggest that life is perhaps not the blessing parents would like to imagine it to be when they are busy inflicting it on others.

One possible explanation for the otherwise bafflingly low rates of suicide among human beings could be that more pleasure is generated by the so-called 'purposeful' activity of *pursuing* pleasure than can be found in the pleasure that is being pursued. If this was the case, however, would one not therefore be committed to arguing that privation is good, since it gives us more to strive for, and therefore more pleasure? This conclusion seems counter-intuitive.*

Perhaps the more likely explanation for our mystifying habit of accepting the gift of life, rather than throwing it back in the faces of those who so generously donated it to us in the first place – on our birthday, appropriately enough – is that the condition of raw aspiration itself provides us with some kind of obscure pleasure. Perhaps, when aspiring, we gain pleasure from the contemplation of those pleasures which we hope to enjoy. Such aspirations may last all day or even all life long, without hiatus.

And so to my investment strategy. The basis of my philosophy is captured in the adage, own what you know and know what you own.† By following this old saw, as a 'small' investor I gain an edge over the institutional investors, and can direct my energies in a highly specific way, cherry-picking the companies I choose to invest in according to what I know about likely future developments in their markets – markets concerning which I have an intimate working knowledge. I can make my investment decisions in my own time, waiting patiently

---

* And would reduce the already vanishingly small figure of 0.00035 to zero, were it not for nocturnal accidents.

† Not to be confused with the maxim, *You are what you own* – which introduces an unnecessary element of ethico-biological confusion into what, strictly speaking, ought to be purely mathematical calculations.

for the right conditions to come about before making a purchase. And because I have no need to justify my decisions to anyone other than myself – am answerable, in short, to my conscience alone – I have no need to realize short-term profits, and thus can stay with the companies I have selected, putting off the moment when I must pay the devil his due (Capital Gains Tax or CGT for short), thus letting my pre-tax profits 'roll over', bringing yet greater growth, until the day of judgement finally comes and the market is forced finally to recognize the underlying value of the companies I own shares in, at which point I sell my equities, realizing some terrific compounded rate of return of, oh, say 25 per cent per annum, thus turning, let us say, £1m into £9,313,225.70 over ten years.*

Technical concerns aside, as you can see, getting rich basically turns on knowing the businesses that you choose to invest in. Now, I knew a bit about philosophy, I knew a bit about cheese, and I knew a bit about skiing. But none of these specialisms seemed very likely to lead to profitable investment opportunities. And so, having finished reading Henri Fox-Farrier's classic in a single sitting, I found myself scratching my head, wondering how exactly I could apply my new-found exper-

---

* Or, for the budget traveller, an equally impressive but perhaps ultimately less satisfying £1 into £9.31.

tise. Then I remembered that I also knew a bit about art.

As an investment vehicle, art has the advantage of being 'fun'.* Furthermore, although one may be obliged to keep in touch with prices currently being achieved at auction and, where possible, in private sales too, artists as such do not submit annual reports, and this factor alone drastically cuts down on the amount of dull preparatory work that the responsible investor might otherwise feel obliged to perform before making his or her rational investment decisions. Hanging around in city centres trying to work out who the key players in the high street are going to be over the coming year is *out*; hanging around in galleries with avant-garde art chicks who divide their time and energy with Germanic scrupulosity between drugs, money, art, and bizarre sex is *in*.

My mind was instantly made up. In the future, my primary source of income would be the profit realized from investing in the works of the big names of tomorrow. No doubt I would occasionally find myself becoming attached to individual works, and thus some-times find it difficult to act with perfect economic

---

* Fun is a depressing word, is it not? To my ear a rotten apple, a slump, or even a death in the family sound more like fun than 'fun' ever does.

rationality.* But just as the great majority of people resist the temptation to sell their children into slavery, so I would no doubt be able to 'treat myself' now and then to such aesthetic indulgences. *Qua* scholar, I would become brilliantly well informed about both the history of art and the contemporary scene; whereas, *qua* connoisseur, my ultimate arbiter of excellence would be my own aesthetic pleasure.

What was more, the nature of the art market fitted precisely with my own theory of value, and made a complete and utter nonsense out of Max's version: everyone knows that the value of a work of art has nothing whatever to do with the number of man-hours that went into its production, and everything to do with the relative rarity and transient desirability of the work itself. Take tinned shit, for instance: highly desirable to collectors, but more or less effortless to produce.† One could probably even devise a theory to calculate the underlying or 'real' value of any particular artist's work, by dividing the aggregate disposable income of the collectors who are interested in that person's output by the total number of works currently in existence.

My spirits were soaring. At last I had found a career that would prove a fitting match for my talents. Aphro

---

* Known technically to economists as 'money grubbing'.
† Depending on the state of the artist's digestion.

– or any woman of exceptional beauty, goodness, and originality – would be proud of me.

I skipped out of my study as though I were dressed in gray shorts, a blazer, and a little green cap. It was early evening. I went out on to the balcony. The sky was blushing with thoughts of night, the river the colour and consistency of slowly congealing blood. On the bridges and along the Embankment commuters limped and stumbled this way and that: confused, suffering, waiting for the silent gunshot that would put them out of their misery once and for all.

I was in a rare mood of contentment.

The sun was sinking, and, perhaps because my metabolism had grown sluggish (my heartbeat was so faint you'd have needed a seismograph to detect it) I quickly found myself shivering with cold.

Still feeling uncannily positive about the world, I went to my room, popped 10 mg Temazepam (the maximum permitted dose) then (fearing yet another night of sleeplessness) took 5 mg extra for good luck. Before ten minutes had elapsed, I was sound asleep.

I woke up shortly afterwards, asphyxiating. Evidently I had fallen so deeply asleep, had left my cares and responsibilities so far behind, that I had even forgotten to breathe. In fact, I still wasn't breathing when I woke up, which struck me as odd, because I nearly always do; in fact, I'd go as far as to say that it's become an instinct with me. But it seemed I had temporarily forgotten how and, try as I might, I could not for the life of me remember the correct technique. I considered shouting out for help, but could not, for my lungs were empty. After ten or fifteen seconds of fascinated panic, I suddenly remembered how it goes: inspire, suspire, pause, repeat.

And so the crisis passed. Safety-conscious as ever, before going back to sleep I gave myself a good talking to, reminding myself that, should I make the same silly, absent-minded mistake again, my future as an art shark would come to nought. Suitably chastened, I let sublime drowsiness drag me back into unconsciousness.

I awoke next morning at what looked suspiciously like dawn. Still drowsy from the sedative I had taken, but surprisingly pleased to find myself still in 'existence', I was aware of having been dreaming, but could not remember what I had been dreaming about. The expression 'fine art' weighed heavily on my tongue, like a challenge or a curse. Suddenly, I realized that I didn't know what it meant. I grabbed a dictionary from my study and took it back to bed with me.

The dictionary defined the phrase as 'those arts which appeal to the intellect or the sense of beauty, including literature and music, and especially painting, sculpture and architecture'. But is the appeal of these arts to the intellect and sense of beauty really sufficient to distinguish them from the performing arts? Or from the liberal arts (the medieval *trivium* of grammar, rhetoric and logic, and the *quadrivium* of arithmetic, geometry, astronomy, and music)? Or from the noble art of self-defence?

'Fine' as opposed to what, then? Crude? Coarse? Shitty? But that can't be what it means because, though critics and artists disagree among themselves about which art is and which art is not crude, coarse and shitty, they certainly do agree that much or even most of it is all of those things. And if you don't believe them, go to your nearest art gallery, where you will undoubtedly find nine out of ten exhibits leave you bored, tired, and regretful for having left the house in the first place.

Then perhaps it is a term of praise, like the word 'poet' in Dylan Thomas's – admittedly partial – view? So an exhibition of fine art would be an exhibition of objects that *aspire* to appeal to our intellects and our senses. But as opposed to what? To the House of Lords, like Mr and Mrs Punchandjudy? To the rules of cricket, like erstwhile administrators of the British Empire, when deciding what particular technique of repression and exploitation to employ in which particular circumstances? And how else can we be entertained *except* by appeal to our intellect and our senses? But then, how am I to decide what to buy?

I fell asleep feeling despondent; my investment career had sputtered out before a mere question of semantics.

I dreamed about a gallery that is exhibiting an enormous custard pie. The proportions of the room in which it is displayed form an almost perfect cube. The custard pie has been cooked in a terrifyingly huge aluminium-foil pie dish. The crinkles around the rim are so sharp that an unwary toddler could easily open their jugular on one of them.

The pie is very yellow, the custard gelatinous and gloppy. It has no crust to speak of – nor is there any browned sugar on top – and the pastry around the rim seems undercooked. In fact, the whole pie seems a little undercooked. Realizing this, I glance nervously at the ceiling, to see if I can spot an electric element, or any other sign that I am in an oven and at risk of being cooked along with the pie. But I am not in an oven, I am in a gallery: the walls and ceiling are painted a uniform white and in one corner an ugly, aggressive little woman dressed in a blue security guard's costume is standing to attention. She is eyeing the pie and me in turn, clearly unable to decide which she finds more distasteful. Without warning, she bares her teeth at me and licks her lips, letting me know that she is hungry and ready to eat if necessary. I look away.

I turn my back on her and begin circumnavigating the pie, strolling and stopping erratically, as one does in galleries, varying the distance between myself and the pie, allowing its various meanings to flicker, catch, and finally burst forth into incandescent realization in consciousness. I picture myself diving in to it fully clothed and swimming lengths through the custard. Then I wonder if the pie is fresh, and the custard still hot; if so, the fulfilment of my sensual wish might well prove fatal.

Suddenly, I find myself surprised and a little annoyed that the pie does not smell of custard. I begin to wonder what the artist is trying to say about the relationship between art object and art consumer. The pie is too large to be consumed, and can therefore only be contemplated; ergo, this work of art forces the hungry consumer into contemplative mode. Also, if the pie is made of real pastry and custard, sooner or later it will go mouldy. This suggestion of ephemerality contradicts our presuppositions about the longevity – the museum-directedness – of art. Because I have begun to enjoy it, I find myself hoping that it will last; but for it to last it must be made from substances far more enduring than pastry and custard. In which case it must be inedible. In which case it is essentially a fake, a *trompe l'oeil* custard pie. Not a custard pie at all, then, but a three-dimensional representation of a custard pie – an imitation pie.

I hunt around the wall for information regarding the materials used in the construction of this piece (the recipe?), but find none. Beset by anxiety, I rack my brains, finally relieving my discomfort by reflecting that, even if it was made of real custard and real pastry, it still would not be a custard pie, because it is too large; no more would a chair that was too large to sit on be a chair in the ordinary sense of the word, but an oversized model or representation of a chair. So what is this piece saying?

The answer comes: *ceci n'est pas une tarte.*

This solution to the puzzle resolves my anxiety and my sense of threat evaporates. Yet at the same time I feel my interest and engagement with the model pie disappear. I am about to walk from the room, dissatisfied by the end of my brief affair with this piece, which I had hoped might flourish into something more permanent and meaningful, when I notice that the security guard has stripped off her uniform to reveal a Fifties-style polka-dot swimming costume and a pale pink bathing cap decorated with rubber 'flowers', and is now standing poised on the rim of the pie, preparing to dive in. She catches my eye and gives me a big, happy grin.

Suddenly I see that she is not at all unattractive. In fact she is rather beautiful, with big pointy breasts, strong straight limbs, and long dark hair, which she had originally pushed up under her bathing cap, but which she now releases, allowing it to tumble sensuously over her neck and shoulders. Flinging the cap aside, a moment later she dives elegantly into the custard, which rises up behind her in a great golden spurt. She surfaces in the centre of the pie, wipes the glistening, sun-coloured liquid from her eyes, and treads custard, still looking and smiling in my direction.

I am dazzled. I look up at the ceiling. The grid of colour-sapping fluorescent lights has now been replaced by a sky of pure azure, across which fluffy white clouds are floating. Looking more carefully, however, I see that the clouds have been painted on pieces of card, and actually glimpse a pair of blue gloves clutching one of the blue-painted sticks on which the clouds are mounted. As far as I can tell, the sky beyond is real.

When I look down again, the custard pool is full of men and women, sporting pleasantly in the liquid. Their figures are voluminous without being fat, as in a painting by Seurat. One couple is playing beach-ball with what appears to be a wedding cake, while elsewhere people of various sexes* engage in sporadic bouts of oral-genital stimulation.

I am overwhelmed with the desire to join the custard party, but feel unsure whether an invitation is necessary. I take off my coat, which anyway feels a little warm in the sunshine. As I do so, a solitary woman catches my eye and, smiling, gestures that I should join her.

---

* My èditor says he can only think of two; but I must remain true to my dream.

I had taken off my shirt and shoes, and was about to remove my trousers, when I woke up.

The answer to my semantic dilemma is on my lips: the fine arts should appeal to the intellect and sense of beauty *as opposed to the passions*. Both artist and connoisseur may be passionate about art, of course; but they must not indulge their passions by means of it.* Shades of sexual desire, anger, pity and fear may well be aroused by art, but only for the sake of contemplation, and never so as to provoke or inhibit action of any kind (other than the signing of cheques, of course). The art lover may covet or revile a painting, but never its subject matter. In other words, art is another country: artists may sell us postcards of the place, but never, ever, are we permitted to visit in person.

Satisfying myself with this hopelessly inadequate and entirely unoriginal solution to the problem, I leaped out of bed. Staggering somewhat – no doubt as a result of the continued influence of the Temazepam, which seems to take about twenty-four hours to wear off – just long enough, in fact, to guarantee that I'll be feeling lively by bedtime – I rebounded off the walls and into the kitchen. While warming up a croissant and gulping down a double espresso, I flicked through a listings magazine to see if there were any interesting shows on. I found one:

---

*   So no wanking over the Rokeby Venus.

an exhibition of installation and film work by a 'hot', up-and-coming young artist, which looked very much like it might be to my taste.

It's already nine-thirty. The dream about the custard pie must have lasted longer than it seemed (perhaps I spent some time unconsciously devising it before actually dreaming it?). The gallery opens at ten. I don't want to miss out on any good investment opportunities, so I rush out of the house, walk briskly along the river, across the footbridge into Charing Cross station, then through Trafalgar Square (where verminous tourists are busy taking photos of the resident pigeons), up on to Piccadilly, and north-west towards Bond Street, where the influential commercial gallery for which I am bound is located.

Unfortunately, though I set off at top speed and full of enthusiasm, by the time I arrive at the gallery I'm utterly exhausted. The effect of the coffee was short-lived, and the Temazepam seems to have taken charge of my metabolism again. The fatigue is such that I'm only vaguely, hazily aware of the purpose of my visit and find myself standing across the road from the gallery, staring blankly at it, very much as if it were an incomprehensible work of contemporary art itself. While I'm gazing at the gallery in this fashion, several people enter and exit, which suggests a lively interest in the artist's work. I can't work out whether I'm pleased about this or not. In the end I turn and stagger back down the street to a coffee shop.

Two espressos later and I'm charged up and ready to hit the exhibition. I breeze through the front door of the gallery and am greeted by a disappointingly spotty female receptionist. She's wearing a bright green dress, against which her boils stand out like forest fruit. But she has a nice (i.e. flirtatious) smile, and I find myself vaguely wondering whether she would be willing to smile on me with other mouths, as she hands me a leaflet about someone called Will Benn, who I can only presume is the artist whose work I have come to admire and possibly purchase. Then she tells me that there are only two exhibits, and points me towards a door.

In the first room, which I have all to myself, I find an installation about time, called *sub specie aeternitatis*, which consists of no fewer than seven hundred and twenty timepieces arranged around the four walls of the room. Each successive chronometer shows a time two minutes 'later' than that displayed by its neighbour, so the room 'contains' twenty-four hours in all. The sequence runs left to right – clockwise from a bird's-eye perspective.

All together, these clocks are making an impressive racket, with strange ripples of reinforced ticking and tocking passing this way and that, as the rhythms of the different mechanisms come into and out of synchronization. But all in all the idea seems rather straightforward and a little dull until – after I have spent several minutes in the room, wondering which way to turn and how on earth I might enjoy this depressingly mundane contraption – one watch in particular catches my eye.

I move towards it. It has wonderfully precise markings, with supplementary dials inset in the main face to account for seconds, tenths and even hundredths of seconds. The impression it makes is very technical and scientific. It is perhaps an astronaut's watch, or a parachutist's watch, if such a thing exists, or perhaps a watch for men who are fired from cannon, which seems even less likely. But it also has an atmosphere of covert activities about it – of abysmal yet perfectly timed crimes committed in the name of progress.

It is, I decide at last, a watch for nuclear bombers – a chrome dome watch. As I am admiring it, and wondering how I might get hold of one myself, I suddenly realize that, along with all the other clocks in the room – grandfather clocks, grandmother clocks, alarm clocks, ship's clocks, half-hunters, chiming watches, nurses' watches, pocket watches, kitchen clocks, and cuckoo clocks – it is running backwards.

I am horrified: why, I do not know. Racking my brains to understand the significance of my discovery, I realize at last that if one locates one of the two clocks which, at any given moment, are telling the 'correct' time, in order to keep in touch with this 'correct' time it is necessary to walk very slowly around the room in a clockwise direction. In other words, in order not to be swept backwards in time, it is necessary continuously to edge in a clockwise direction at the rate of one clock a minute, completing a circuit of the room once in every twelve hours. And yet perhaps edging forwards is not enough. For many of the clocks have second hands. And so, if you wanted to be really precise, and not allow things to slip for so much as a moment – which I for one would not – you would have to hare round the room once every minute, each time ending up at the next clock in the series.

But which side of the room is night and which day?

This god-sized conundrum induces in me a strong gust of nausea, a modicum of anger towards the artist, together with a rapid increase in my feeling of tiredness. I can't be bothered to work out what it might mean. All I know is the disparate sounds of ticking are gradually becoming deafening, and I can feel myself beginning to move in time to them. Someone is trying to turn me into a clock, and I desperately don't want this to happen. And so, before I get stuck there for ever, attempting to solve the philosophical puzzle of time with my own body, I stagger through the door into the next room, letting out a great sigh of relief as I go.

The next room is set up to show a film – Exhibit

Number Two. Plain, white, box-construction benches with hemp-coloured cushions are arrayed in perfectly straight lines in front of a small silver screen. Nothing is showing at present. On the benches, half a dozen people are variously murmuring to one another, staring into space, looking at their watches, and reading the handout they received from Holly Bush at the door.

As I sit there yawning and taking deep breaths, in spite of myself I find I am wondering about *sub specie aeternitatis*. One problem I have with the piece, apart from the fact that it very nearly caused me to suffer a psychotic breakdown, is that much the same effect could have been achieved without having the clocks running at all. If each clock was set to show a time one minute after the preceding clock, each clock would be right once a day, and the position of the 'right' clock would move around the room once every twelve hours. Day and night would not be present simultaneously – but then, they aren't, are they?

The way the artist has arranged things does have the benefit of the combined ticking of seven hundred and twenty chronometers, which is a powerful effect. But what about accuracy? After all, no clock keeps perfect time. Won't the whole machine be out of kilter within months?

While meditating on the notion of accuracy, it suddenly dawns on me that what the artist has done is even more diabolical than I first realized. Because each clock is travelling backwards, the moment at which the time shown by any one of them coincides with 'real' time is infinitesimally small. This means that, were one to accept the implicit invitation and spend a day or two circling the room, attempting to stay in the present rather than being swept away into the past or accelerating into the future, unless one's movements were unimaginably precise one would constantly find oneself not where time is, that is to say, in the present – but rather where it is about to be or has just been.

Though this realization should come as some relief to me, suggesting as it does that numerical concepts of time are illusory, instead a fresh gust of nausea sweeps over me. The man sitting in front of me is staring at his watch, clicking his fingers in time to the second hand. Finding myself beginning to panic, I change seats so that I can no longer see him. Taking deep breaths, I resolve there and then to stop exploring the ramifications of *sub specie aeternitatis* once and for all.

Instead, to calm myself down, I debate with myself whether or not I should buy it. But far from calming me down, as the prospect of getting out my credit card usually does, this idea seems quite as insane as the work itself, and causes me just as much perplexity. Thankfully, before I have time to explore the pros and cons in any detail, the room lights dim, the hidden projector flickers into life, and the silver screen is illuminated.

Partially framed by a string of light bulbs that decorate the entrance arch and ticket office, we see the big top of a circus. In the distance, beyond the big top, are some mature horse-chestnut and oak trees, and beyond them a road, on which a little traffic can be seen. Reality is speeded up in the film, which must have been made using time-lapse techniques, so occasionally, when someone wanders across the screen (to open up the shutters that cover the front of the mobile box office, or twiddle with an electrical connection) they move too quickly, as when movies shot on older, slower cameras are shown on modern projectors running at twenty-four frames per second.

The people who are setting up the box office and lights and the people who are putting the finishing touches to the big top itself are dressed very casually and move with a kind of slovenly, workmanlike distaste for activity, which is visible in their comportment even though they're moving faster than they should.

After about five minutes (our time) of such sporadic comings and goings, the white lights come on. They look like strings of pearls. Finally, the box office is opened for business, and everyone but the two women who run it disappears from view. After an interval of several minutes, during which we are treated to the sight of the box-office women smoking cigarettes with joyous speed and precision, a group of prospective punters gathers at the box office, wondering whether or not to buy tickets. They choose not to. Then another group appears.

This lot know exactly what they want. Four adults and about seven children, all looking equally excited, buy tickets at the box office, mill around for a while beneath the pearly lights, then walk off down the greasy, grassy avenue that leads directly to the big top, where their tickets are checked by a man in a dark leather jacket who lurks on the threshold of the big top's shadowy interior. The punters cross the threshold and are immediately engulfed in darkness. Meanwhile, more people are showing up at the box office. Some must have already purchased their tickets, because they file straight through the illuminated gateway.

The camera remains fixed throughout, so sometimes the screen is clotted with bodies, cruelly blocking our view of the longed-for big top. It is autumn, and an occasional squall causes the fallen leaves to whirl round in circles. When this happens, people pull down their hats and draw their collars up to keep their necks warm. Most people are happy and excited. Others look dutiful.

Others exhibit no emotion, as if circuses, hospital waiting rooms, restaurants, morgues, bookie's shops and swimming pools were all one to them.

More people arrive; a queue forms at the box office, and the excitement of the crowd starts to feed on itself. Even though the film is speeded up, it's only running at 110 per cent or perhaps 120 per cent of the speed of reality (the speed of reality – what the fuck is that? 24 fps? one revolution per day? 68 heartbeats per minute? I'm feeling disturbed, and begin to wonder if I've been permanently traumatized by the previous exhibit). So the build-up to whatever is about to happen in this circus, fascinating though it may be, is just a little more gradual than I can take in my current state of mind and, ever so slowly, ever so imperceptibly (at around 60 per cent of the speed of reality, and eventually, in the final stages, at around 25 per cent) I fall asleep.

I awake with a horrible start, jerking upright just as I am about to pitch forwards off my chair. I grunt loudly, which makes most of the other people in the room turn and look at me in confusion. I too am looking around in confusion. But my confusion is not so great that I do not notice that the man who was sitting in front of me before I moved is *still* staring at his watch. He's stopped clicking his fingers, presumably out of consideration to the other gallery-goers, but is now holding the dial right up to his eye, counting out the seconds, unblinking.

On the screen I am disappointed to see the pearly gate has not only been switched off, but is actually being dismantled. The portable box office has gone and the big top itself is in the process of being deflated and cleared away. My heart sinks. How could I let myself miss the dénouement? I was so excited by the piece! I certainly felt far better disposed towards it than the neo-psychotic *sub specie aeternitatis*. I've always loved the idea of circuses* and would very much like to own a work of art that takes as its subject matter their supernatural allure.

I watch in a state of profound yet fascinated disappointment as the big top is slowly folded up and loaded on a truck. Gradually, all the equipment is packed away and one by one the convoy of trucks and mobile homes that house the circus and its stars drive off, churning up the grass as they go. We are left with a lingering shot of the park, now deserted, looking distinctly muddy and banal. Occasionally, a solitary leaf flits across the screen. At one point a little flurry of leaves actually seems to be attacking the camera, like a mob of disgruntled political protesters. In the distance, the cars that are

---

* I've never actually been to one; I imagine they must be tawdry places inside, full of depressed animals and disillusioned children.

creeping around the park's boundary road now have their headlights on. A queue of traffic forms at a junction. For a moment, everything is perfectly still. Then the film ends.

I am absolutely thrilled by this piece, and feel very tempted to rush back to the reception area and whip out my credit card right away. But I succeed in reining in my enthusiasm, telling myself that I'd be a fool to buy a piece of art that I haven't yet succeeded in watching from beginning to end without nodding off half-way through. I consider asking the man who is holding his watch up against his right eye how long the film ran for, but I'm afraid that were I to cause him to lose count he might lash out at me, so I look at my leaflet instead: forty-five minutes. So I can't have missed much of it. I mull over the problem in my mind, and eventually decide that the rational thing to do is to go and take some cocaine, then come back and watch the film again.

In the gallery entrance I ask Holly whether there is a toilet in the building that I might use. She indicates a door, which is difficult to spot because it is painted in white emulsion, like the wall around it, and has no handle and no frame. I pass through this door into a dark corridor, where I find another door standing ajar. Inside I see a lavatory.

Locking the door behind me, I search the lining of my jacket, down at the hem where substances accumulate, an invaluable resource in case of emergencies such as this one. Happily, I find a handful of dried mushrooms, about three-quarters of a gram of coke and a huge number of 'slimming' tablets that I occasionally buy mail order from the US. They're actually speed, presumably working on the principle that if you're incapable of sitting, standing or lying still for more than five seconds at a time you're bound to burn up a little more energy than usual, and hopefully in this way will lose weight. I gobble down twelve of these tablets, which are really very small and innocuous-looking. Then I start fumbling around with the cocaine, which is in one of those natty little folded paper pouches that Trog sometimes makes up for me.

Because the amphetamine has yet to have any effect, and the Temazepam is still impairing my coordination, I end up spilling the cocaine over the cistern and lavatory lid (which, thankfully, I remembered to close before I began). Rather than mess around trying to gather it together and cut it with a credit card, I decide instead – rather recklessly as it happens – simply to stick a twenty up my nose and hoover the stuff up wherever I can find it.

Five minutes later, having explored every surface and crevasse of the toilet with my twenty-pound tube, and having sucked up some unpalatably large lumps of coke in the process (as well as a lot of germs and probably a few pubic hairs too), my nose and throat are burning and my eyes are streaming with tears. Still, I'm very definitely buzzed, and feeling quietly confident that I will not fall asleep during the second showing of my film.

Before leaving the toilet I am faced with the choice of returning the mushrooms to the hem of my jacket, flushing them down the toilet, or eating them. For the sake of convenience, I opt for the latter course. As always, they taste disgusting.

I leave the toilet and emerge back into the foyer. Holly takes one look at me, grins in recognition, and asks me if I've got any left and if she can have some. I shake my head, unable to speak because of the stinging in my nose, throat and trachea. Holly looks seriously disappointed. I manage to mutter 'sorry', before striding towards the glass door that leads into the street. Realizing too late that I've gone in the wrong direction, I decide that I ought to display the courage of my convictions, and continue walking until I reach the café where I had coffee earlier that day.

Caffeine is the last thing I need now but, in order to wash away some of the cocaine that has adhered to my mucous membranes, and to get the vile taste of those mushrooms out of my mouth, I order a Diet Coke.

Half-way through the Diet Coke I'm beginning to feel

so excited that I find it very difficult to remain seated. My legs are bouncing up and down with a life of their own, and I'm chewing my teeth as if they were fruit drops. Remembering that I have a spliff in my breast pocket, I leap violently from my seat and charge towards the toilet, which is located at the back of the café. Safely lodged inside, I take out the spliff – which, again, is for emergency use only, composed as it is of 75 per cent grass and 25 per cent hash – light it, and smoke it in three minutes flat.

When I emerge from the lavatory I pay at the counter, leaving the bemused waitress a twenty, and head straight back to the gallery. Ignoring Holly, who looks longingly at me as I pass (I know her type: it's not love, it's drugs she's after), I walk through *sub specie aeternitas* with my eyes closed and my hands over my ears. After banging into the opposite wall, I feel my way into the projection room, where I open my eyes again. The room is fuller than it was last time; it's lunchtime, and a number of people who work for a living appear to have come to check out what all the fuss is about.

The film hasn't started yet. I look for a place on one of the crowded benches. In the end I find myself sitting down between a balding American tourist and an attractive woman in her early thirties, who has brown, shoulder-length hair, and a shiny green overcoat that is obviously made out of some nasty synthetic fabric, but which I cannot help thinking would feel as soft as silk were I to stroke it with the back of my hand.

Though full, the room is almost perfectly silent; it is even possible to hear ticking coming from the next room. The room lights are up, and the silver screen itself is a brilliant white void. I'm gnawing at my teeth like a horse with a mouthful of sugar lumps, and my heart is pounding as if I'd just had a near-life experience. My eyes are taking everything in so quickly, are darting round the room in such a frenzy, that the world has started to look like a kind of cubist movie – an arrangement of surfaces that have been detached from their objects and are being shuffled in space by some demonic card sharp.

In an attempt to calm down I start a silent conversation with myself. I am sitting down, I say to myself, and I am in an art gallery. Ergo, I am sitting down in an art gallery. Good. The woman to my right is wearing green, and the man to my left is bald. Ergo, I am sitting down in an art gallery between a balding man and a greening woman. Is the woman perchance greening for the man? Is the man perchance greening for his hair? It is certainly possible. Good.

An unbearable tension rises, rises. Movement is absolutely necessary and absolutely impossible. The waiting is unbearable. The film might not come on for another, oh, two or even three minutes. I cannot, simply cannot remain seated. I seriously consider standing up in front of this audience of lunchtime Apollonians and singing a song; if I had any kind of voice at all I would probably do so. But my voice is execrable, so instead of a sing-song I decide to have a screamscream. Screaming is f-u-n, I say to myself.

I am about to let rip, but before the 'go' signal has travelled from my brain to my mouth I have become bored with the idea. Instead, I find myself fascinated once again by the woman's shiny green coat, which is, I feel sure, made from one of the softest, most sensual fabrics known to man; it only looks shiny so that people are thrown off the scent, and the woman can walk the streets without being mobbed by people who are crazed with the desire to caress and stroke her.

I am about to reach out and touch her arm when I realize what a dull proposition even the softest fabric is, compared with the idea of throttling the balding American to my left. But his wife, who is sitting to his left, would be bound to object, so I reject the idea on the grounds that it is likely to cause a scene.

At this point I realize that, if I don't say something to someone *now*, my head is actually going to explode into fragments. I'm not about to start talking to the bald guy, whom I loathe, so the obvious candidate is the incredibly textured woman. I don't want her to think I'm trying to pick her up, though, so I need to think of something to say that doesn't sound like a chat-up line.

I have an idea. I've still got most of my hair, so I turn to her and ask loudly, without any presumption of intimacy, 'All things being equal, do you find bald men more or less attractive than men who still have all their hair?' She looks at me, looks at my hair, sees that it is mostly still there, and is absolutely stumped. In a world that has lost its capacity for wonder, I feel gratified by the effect my question has on this woman. At the same time, I feel the man on my left stiffening and, from out of the corner of my eye, can just see his wife leaning forward in order to find out who is insulting her husband in public.

My interlocutor is saved from having to think up some suitably neutral answer to my staggeringly pene-trating question because, the very next moment, the room lights begin to dim. She smiles at me – indulgently, I think – and turns to face the screen.

The benches are now full to bursting; people sit stiffly, anchored to their seats, focusing on the screen like jewellers searching for imperfections in a gem. My heart is pounding in my head. The film begins.

About ten seconds later (the first customer has just waddled comically across the screen towards the box office) I can bear it no longer; I feel as though I've been sitting in that room for generations. Each of the twenty-four frames that rebounds from the screen every second feels like a drop of peculiarly heavy liquid landing on my forehead – the fine-art equivalent to the Chinese water torture.

Without so much as a hint of any conscious intention to do so, I find myself leaping from my seat. The distance between myself and the aisle is about nine feet; the distance from there to the door at least another twelve. The square of the hypotenuse of a right-angled triangle is equal to the sum of the squares of the two remaining sides, and the answer flashes up into my brain: *it's a three-four-five triangle*. Just as this answer appears I find myself leaping across the benches, keeping to the hypotenuse with a stringency that obliges me to knock off an elderly man's spectacles and dislodge a well-dressed teenage girl from her seat, depositing her on the floor.

In the foyer I pass the jagged, futuristic-looking Holly Bush and scream something at her about taking a call from Pythagoras. A nanosecond or two later I am streaking down the street, heading who knows where. I finally come to rest in Trafalgar Square, sweating heavily, where I become entranced by the pigeons, which are far more colourful and variegated than is usually apparent. The tourists, on the other hand, are dressed in identical red and yellow waterproofs. Each face wears the same inscrutable smile, and they repel me as never before.

I sit on a stone step, asking myself over and over how I am feeling. Again and again I ask myself, but no answer is forthcoming. I feel nothing. But, feeling nothing, however am I to decide what to do next? The anxiety builds and I begin to panic. Then I realize that I have reached nirvana. A mushroom-cloud of pleasure erupts and I gasp with delight. I close my eyes. All is colour. All is white.

'I feel nothing,' I hear myself murmur ecstatically.

Then I open my eyes again and look up at the sky, which is the most fabulous tone of gray, and at Nelson's column, which is so tall that Nelson himself seems rather diminutive, and putting him high up on a column appears to me a hilarious joke, a gloriously telling piece of civic ambivalence towards outstanding individual achievement. Then all the strength drains from my limbs and torso and I have to lie down. A moment later I find myself vomiting. I watch out of the corner of my eye as the vomit – which contains several undigested blue pills, one or two shapes which could be dried mushrooms, and a surprisingly large volume of Diet Coke, which is actually still fizzy – dribbles and flows down the steps. A likeable Japanese couple take a photograph of me.

When I feel that I am ready to move again, I climb uneasily to my feet and wander down Northumberland Avenue towards the Embankment. I pass a wedding shop, with its grotesque parodies of purity displayed braggingly in the window; the Sherlock Holmes pub, with its manifold references to that grotesque nine-teenth-century parody of rationality; a gold Rolls-Royce that has been wheel-clamped, which I take to be a grotesque parody of transportation; and a reflection of myself, which I take to be a grotesque parody of humanity. A little further on, beneath the arches of the Embankment railway bridge, I come across what appears to be a sub-aqua diving shop.

I have never noticed this before and stop to look in the window, wondering about the fabulous undersea creatures that only those willing and brave enough to don these brightly coloured rubber suits will ever clap eyes upon (or be stung, bitten, electrocuted or eaten by).

The idea of buying one of these outfits and plung-ing into the dense, gray waters of the Thames appeals enormously. What might I find down there, amongst the silt and the trash? What ghoulish figures might I discover, lurking on the river bed, waving as they sway this way and that with the ebb and flow of the tide, boots embedded in concrete, mushy flesh parting from grimy bone like the meat of some overcooked fowl?

Brussels – I suddenly remember, apropos of nothing – bricked over its river years ago, hence the unusual preponderance of child sex murderers, etcetera, that city harbours. I find myself taking out my mobile phone to book a table for supper at my favourite Belgian restaurant, while at the same time making a dash for the Eurostar Terminal. After three paces I come to a halt.

Stay in London, I tell myself. Stay in London, where each and every citizen is free to stand on any one of London's many bridges and look out for the vast number of corpses that float by every day, unseen by tourists. Corpses are invisible to tourists; it takes a truly independent traveller to spot them.

In the vain hope of calming myself down I stagger into Embankment underground station, with the intention of taking the tube to Charing Cross. Charing Cross is further from my flat than Embankment, but I often find shuffling through the tunnels and escalators of a decent-sized tube station – being cursed for getting in people's way and cursing them in return for getting in mine – a curiously calming, even moving experience, and I hope to benefit from that effect now.

The human interaction; the human colour; the nostalgic effect of architectural details that have remained in place for fifty or even a hundred years; the bitter mundanity of the creaky old trains and their graffiti-mangled décor; the human filth; the posters attempting to lure commuters to this or that putrid entertainment; the weird sense of being caught up in some civic circulatory system; the shared feeling of being on your way somewhere: on a good day, if such can be imagined, these factors combine to produce a powerful sense of –

without wishing to overstate my case in any way – a powerful sense of . . . of travelling by tube.

On this occasion, however, I experience a new effect. As I am wandering down a long, narrow corridor towards the northbound Bakerloo platform – vaguely surprised by the similarity between walking somewhat giddily through this grubby, pale-blue-tiled tunnel and accelerating to the speed of light on an arcade video game I spent an afternoon and about £50 playing earlier in the week – I suddenly notice a poster, a little larger than usual, standing out on the right-hand side of the tunnel.

The poster is square, which is unusual in itself, and appears to be advertising a modern-art exhibition. The work they have chosen to feature on the poster is highly abstract, consisting of a perfectly symmetrical grid of what seem to be irregularly shaped but basically square biscuits. The biscuits are large and somewhat mangled, as if someone had nibbled at each one before cementing it to the canvas. The canvas and the biscuits are of more or less the same colour, and between the biscuits proper are smaller particles of biscuit – crumbs as it were – which have also adhered to the canvas. The texture of the canvas itself is not visible through the mass of biscuit and cement. The colour varies between straw for the biscuits, with patches of earth brown and black, and a paler, whiter version of the same for the cement.

I step backwards to admire this reproduction of what is undoubtedly an important work, and which is quite unlike anything I have ever seen before. The combination of perfect regularity in the spacing of the 'biscuits' and the utter chaos of their setting produces a really powerful aesthetic emotion in me. This, I think to myself, is a work I could live with. Who might the artist be?

A few people – tourists, worker bees, I don't notice which – push past me, obscuring my view. When they have passed I start looking around for the part of the poster that will tell me where the exhibition is, but can't find it anywhere.

That's when I realize that I'm not looking at a poster, but a section of blue-tiled wall which a workman, for reasons known only to people who maintain tunnels for a living, has attacked with a cold chisel or some such implement, carefully removing each tile and leaving behind only the yellowish-brown clumps of cement which once held it in place.

Suddenly I find myself standing in an underground tunnel staring appreciatively at a section of wall. A man with a briefcase approaches. I am acutely aware that this man has already decided, from a distance of around five or six metres, that I am completely insane. He is not all that nervous, however; presumably because I am well dressed – more expensively so than he is, in fact. As he walks past me he simply averts his eyes. I remain rooted to the spot, too embarrassed to go any further along the tunnel in case I bump into one or more of the people who have already observed my crazed behaviour. Not that they will mind, of course; I have been living in London too long to imagine that anyone gives a damn if they happen to pass a well-dressed connoisseur of underground maintenance work lurking in a tunnel. But I do not wish to be ignored in the precise way those people will now ignore me; I am feeling too susceptible to suggestion, and could too easily find myself believing that what those averted eyes say about me is true.

I resurface, cross the river by the footbridge (overcoming without difficulty the temptation to throw myself into the angry swirling waters of the Thames), then trip lightly along the Embankment towards my flat.

Outside the Royal Festival Hall I bump into Rosa, an old girlfriend. We greet each other politely – we parted on good terms – and I ask her casually if she has any idea why there are tears streaming down my face. She seems surprised by my question, though it is obvious to me that she has already noticed the tears, which was why I asked her in the first place. She quickly recovers herself and informs me, with a hint of fatigue or perhaps even aggression in her voice, that I am crying because both my parents died in an aircrash when I was a child and I still haven't faced up to the fact, let alone begun to get over it.

I thank her politely for her suggestion, but tell her that I am sure she is mistaken. I wonder to myself why it is women always read so much significance into such things, and come to the conclusion that it is a sort of power play on their part; knowing as they do that when a man is upset it is invariably to a woman he will turn for comfort, they do everything in their power to exaggerate such trivial symptoms of disquiet.

We exchange pleasantries and then say goodbye, promising, fingers crossed behind our backs, that we will ring one another soon.

The sun comes out; shining is hardly the word.

Feeling warmly unemotional and exceptionally objective, I set off briskly along the bank of the Thames, watching its smooth blue water sweep eagerly towards the sea where, freed from the antipathetic logic of earth, which forces it to run in channels, it parties day and night with its friends the waves, governed only by the moods of the moon.

When I arrive home, the blind man to whom I donated fifty pounds in a drunken fit of charitable giving a few days earlier is staring at me even more intently than usual. Did the fifty offend him? Or has he still not forgiven me for that awkward incident when, in a cunning attempt to prove that far from being blind, this man possesses not just normal but in fact extraordinarily *acute* eyesight, I threw a crumpled-up tenner at him? As it happened, my experiment failed; the tenner hit him on the nose and rebounded some distance off, and I was obliged to pick it up, smooth it flat, and hand it back to him. I'm still not completely convinced he isn't putting on an act to whip up pity for himself. After all, it would hardly be worth breaking cover for a tenner, would it?

(even more expedition finances)

When I arrived back from my art-collecting expedition, Aphro was not at home. I showered, threw my vomit-spattered shirt in the bin, then attempted to eat some breakfast cereal. But my body did not want it. I myself was indifferent, so I did not press the point.

It was only two o'clock, but I felt as wired and tired as any city trader who's been striking billion-dollar deals from dawn till dusk. Furthermore, in spite of not having actually purchased anything, I felt rather proud of the amount of raw energy I had put into my first day's collecting. Striding about my flat, I once again began to wonder about the circus film. I retrieved the leaflet Holly Bush had given me and attempted to read it in detail. My eyes weren't focusing well, and my mind wasn't focusing well either, but after about half an hour I managed to glean that, shortly after the punters troop into the big top, the thing is deflated, folded away, and the whole circus leaves town. The punters themselves are never seen again.

So maybe I hadn't fallen asleep for more than a few seconds. But where did all the people go? I lay on a chaise longue for about two hours, staring through the window at the sky, wondering about those people, and all the fun they either did or did not have, and where they might be now. Is it good to be trapped for ever in a circus? Is it a punishment? I reflected on my own life for guidance, but found it difficult to unlock the metaphor in any convincing fashion.

Even so, I decide that I am a great admirer of Will Benn's work, and resolve to go back to the gallery tomorrow and purchase both pieces. I even consider commissioning him to create the gargantuan custard pie I dreamed about that morning, but on reflection decide that it might be a bit presumptuous to do so; after all, the patronage relationship no longer works like it used to, when artists were unliveried servants, barely superior to writers and trash of that kind, and therefore obliged to create to order whatever tickled their employer's fancy.

The various kinds of high that I have been suffering since my trip to the gallery seem to be wearing off, and I'm left feeling mashed, both inside and out. Inevitably, my thoughts turn to my new employee. The flat seems to be in good order, the kitchen is clean and tidy, so I can't think of anything to complain about. But where is she? Suspecting that she may be in the flat after all, working silently at her desk, I wander over to her room and knock gently on the door. No answer. I hesitate for a few moments, then open the door a few inches and peek inside in order to make sure that she is genuinely absent, taking good care not to look at any of her possessions (particularly not the photographs of her family), or to notice any alterations she may or may not have made to the arrangement of the furniture, etcetera (she has made none). Then I check her bathroom (scrupulously averting my eyes from her scant selection of inexpensive toiletries), just in case she has committed suicide. No one there either.

I go back into the living room and pour myself a tumbler of nice, light Speyside malt whisky, diluted with a teaspoonful of mineral water to take away the burn. This calms me and settles my stomach. I sit down by the broad expanse of window in my original Arne Jacobsen black-leather swivel armchair and stare out across London. Several cranes, erected to help with the various construction projects that are constantly going on in this great inorganic lichen they call a city, are penetrating and otherwise defacing the skyline. These cranes, I realize, are spoiling my view. I didn't buy a flat with a view over the Thames and the West End in order to look at cranes. My anger flares. I paid for this view, and

I cannot see why other people should have the right to mar it in any way.

My mind begins to focus on this problem – perhaps as a direct result of my aesthetically over-stimulating morning. Gradually, it focuses harder and harder. Very soon, the tension is unbearable, and I grab the phone and ring Westminster Council, who sympathize but tell me that new building work is essential to the continued prosperity of the city, and they cannot do anything to help me.

Next I ring a graphics company, to enquire how much it would cost to have the windows papered over with a high resolution image of the relevant part of the city, digitally doctored to remove the bits I don't like. To my surprise they take my enquiry seriously. This unequivocal sign that the person on the other end of the line is as mad as I am makes me distrust the company they work for, and I secretly decide to take my business elsewhere. Nevertheless, I continue to converse with them for the sake of politeness. After all, I'm not talking to a cold caller (who in my opinion are simply asking – pleading, even – for robust verbal abuse).

After further discussions we decide that the most effective solution would be to print out the image on transparent film, which we would then have sandwiched between two layers of glass. The glass thus formed could then be put in place of the glass I currently have, which is of the plain 'see-through' variety. In this way both the living room and, as it were, the view itself would continue to be illuminated by natural light.

I hold the line for five minutes while the helpful maniac I am talking to makes some quick calculations. The ball-park figure they quote me is astronomical, which makes me realize why they took my enquiry seriously in the first place: no one in their right mind would turn down such a lucrative contract. Satisfied that I am dealing with a sane human being after all, I tell them I'll ring them back once I've decided whether I want St Paul's Cathedral in or out.

I put the phone down and continue staring out of the window, placated by the thought that if the cranes – or St Paul's Cathedral for that matter – ever really do become too much for me, I will be able to take immediate remedial action.

I knock back another half-pint tumbler of malt whisky and am rewarded by a sudden hallucination: a choir of angels falls out of the sky, laughing till their sides split at this world that they've abandoned. They land in the river one after another, only to re-emerge moments later with their wings, cloaks, and various bits of gilded apparatus wholly unsullied by the fecal-hued waters. I'm actually looking at seagulls. I know I'm looking at seagulls. But why, if I want to see angels, should I be limited to seagulls? Who says I must? Who sets these rules? I, for one, have no intention of abiding by them. For I am rich.

Close to tears, I spring out of my seat, shuffle to my room, chew down 15 mg of Temazepam, which I find difficult to swallow because my throat is so dry, then crawl under my duvet – fully clothed – where I twitch pleasantly, and hug myself. After some indistinct span of time that lies somewhere between five minutes and five hours, I drift off into a light coma and dream about walking up a long flight of stairs that leads to a closed door. I make multiple trips up and down this staircase, being encouraged after each successive failure by various gallery owners, stair sweepers, passers-by, 'friends', and members of my family (I don't have one) to give the door one more try.

When I awake I can hear someone in the kitchen. Without thinking, like a man with a mission – like a doctor on call, or a fighter pilot responding to the scramble signal – I leap out of bed, tear off my clothes, put on my pyjamas and dressing gown (so as not to let on that I have been sleeping in an eight-hundred-pound suit), and wander into the kitchen, where I find Aphro making herself a cup of tea.

She turns to me and smiles. I guess I must look pretty ragged, because I detect in her eye a whisper of consternation. She offers me a cup of tea, which I accept.

One of the things I have noticed about Aphro since

she moved into my flat approximately eighty-four hours ago is her silence, which I find both profoundly troubling and devastatingly charming. It makes me angry; I want to ruffle it, to make it vibrate, to turn it into noise. Her silence is like the skin of a drum, or some other beautiful instrument which begs to be played. But I am acutely aware that I have no idea how to get a note out of this instrument, and am terrified to try, lest I only succeed in producing some screeching, throbbing, wailing, sobbing, groaning noise, such as I am wont to make when I am feeling musical.

There seems to be an almost ungovernable amount of silence in the room at the moment, and this silence is in danger of speaking. In order to prevent it from doing so, I step into the breach and start talking. I listen to what I have to say with at least as much interest as Aphro shows, and possibly even more astonishment; I've certainly no more idea than she has what's coming next.

'Well, yes, it's probably about time we got things straightened out between us. The first thing I'd like to say is that I'm very pleased how well our arrangement is working out. The flat is, I have to say, absolutely immaculate, and your kindness in making me the odd cup of tea and the occasional snack is much appreciated. Because of your help I was able to spend a very productive morning checking out some rather exciting investment opportunities, and am considering making a purchase tomorrow.

'The second thing I'd like to say is probably not necessary, but just to set your mind at rest – and that's very important to me because I stand to benefit as much as you do from your continued happiness and contentment in your new . . . position – so what I'd like to say is that, well, I know that someone of your standard . . . of physical attractiveness – if I can say that without prejudice to our eminently non-sexual employer-employee relationship – your physical attractiveness and your intelligence and your diligence in performing your . . . responsibilities . . . and your . . . yes – your silence . . . above all, your silence – I know very well that someone with all these qualities would never, ever, ever find someone like me, who is both older and richer and far unhappier than herself, at all attractive – and therefore I'd just like to say that I think we should keep things on the footing we've established. I'll be going away at the end of next week and probably will not be back for, oh, six months. No tea for me actually, I'm just about ready for bed, as you can see, thank you.'

Unaware of precisely what it is I have just revealed, I am only too conscious of the look of pain and confusion that has gripped Aphro's usually placid features. As she opens her mouth to speak I spin around and dive through the kitchen door. Moving as fast as my legs will carry me, I dart into my own room then through into my *en suite* bathroom, where I turn on the shower and, without bothering to remove either my pyjamas or my dressing gown, step into the scalding hot water and begin scrubbing myself vigorously, with moisturizing soap and a genuine sea sponge.

Another abstract period of time later (which I will not even attempt to specify, since this is a qualitative study of the gentle art of independent travel, and is not intended by any manner or means to be interpreted as purporting to contain information of quantitative or statistical significance), during which I try and fail miserably to have an orgasm, I am lying in bed, having removed my night clothes and put on my jogging kit (minus running shoes, of course; I loathe self-conscious eccentricity), when there is a quiet knock on the door. Astonished, I ask the mystery visitor to come in.

It is Aphro (how strange, I almost said Gaia). She is looking really quite scared, standing on the threshold as though she has just found herself in a magical fairytale world, where rooms have a significance which altogether transcends their floor plan, ceiling height, and décor. Since she does not speak, I break the ice by asking her if I can help her in any way.

She takes the cue, telling me that she was a little worried about me because I seemed rather upset, and wonders whether she can do anything for me.

'I keep unusual hours, you mean?' I ask her.

She looks puzzled. No, she tells me, that is not what she meant.

'Then what exactly is the problem?' I demand, attempting to sound authoritative.

'You seemed really upset, and I wondered if I could help,' she repeats, still hovering on the threshold, as if forewarned by a benevolent wizard that to cross into the room itself would result in her shrinking to a fraction of her former size.

By way of response, I sigh and explain to her in a perfunctory tone that I bumped into a friend earlier, who insisted on dredging up some unpleasant memories from my past, which had disturbed me. In a further effort to shut her up, I compliment her on her sensitivity in noticing my disquiet. The effect of these patronizing words is completely undermined when Aphro laughs dryly, and remarks that even an invertebrate would have found it difficult to miss the signs.

We stare at each other in silence for a few moments, before I finally put an end to the conversation by smiling warmly, saying goodnight, rolling over to face the other way, and turning out my bedside lamp.

(a journey to another world)

There is nothing more utterly transporting than a good night's sleep, especially when it is topped off with a generous helping of sweet dreams. Indeed, I am reliably informed that there are people on this planet who have been so impressed by what happens or appears to happen to them when they are sleeping that they are of the fixed belief that the world of dreams, which we enter (if we are lucky) when we sleep (again, if we are lucky), is more real than the world of sticks and stones and broken bones we inhabit during our so-called 'waking' hours.

Yet for all that, speaking as a chronic insomniac, whose natural streak of independence makes him resent the condition of abject impotence in which we wait for Sleep to collect us at bedtime and then drop us off again at the end of the night, I find I have mixed feelings. It has been said that Sleep comes softly and is sweet for men, while his brother, Death, approaches with violence and is terrible. But I myself thoroughly dislike the way the great somnificator steals up on you, touching you on the forehead with a bit of branch (his so-called 'wand'), or pouring a soporific into your ear from his little horn, or sprinkling sleepy dust in your eyes,* before embracing you and carrying you off to dreamland. I find this way of carrying on surreptitious, shifty, and even, at times, downright malicious.†

I believe it is my dislike of Sleep's methods that led me to adopt the habit of sitting, lying or standing for hours on end, waiting anxiously for his arrival, frigid with fear lest he should not show, yet at the same time determined not to let him make a fool of me yet again. My secret hope was that I might be fully conscious and cogent when he turned up, so that I might question him about his methods, give him a piece of my mind regarding the shabby way he had treated me in the past, and thus encourage him to play fairly and openly with me in future. I was also keen to have a word with him

---

* Or whatever it is he actually does – I don't know because (somewhat paradoxically) I've always fallen asleep before I can work out what in God's name is going on.
† I am thinking of those cases when he repeatedly taps you on the forehead with his wand, then jolts you awake a moment later. Worse still are the occasions when he takes you into his arms and sweeps you up into the air, only to drop you back on to your mattress from ceiling height, juddering into consciousness, your heart pounding and your throat dry.

about my dreams. Because the ones I was having at the time really did not bear repeating, yet I had them again and again.

And if my attitude to sleep suggests to you that I was an excessively self-conscious creature, who resented the least derogation from my ability consciously to control my mental state and processes, I would agree whole-heartedly with you, only adding by way of mitigation that, while it was true that I lived my life like a rabbit in headlights, with all the unselfconscious joy and instinc-tual freedom of action this image implies, at least I was fully aware of the problem, and strived with all the power and determination of my conscious will to allay it, by loosening up, analysing things less, taking deep breaths, taking things as they come, taking it easy, taking drugs, always being one of the first people to start dancing at parties, chilling out, enjoying myself, relaxing, being laid back, getting it together, getting it on, getting a life, and being happy.

But to return to the subject from which I have just strayed. On those odd occasions when I did succeed in sleeping, and found myself in that other world, where the constraints which physical reality puts on our fantasy life no longer apply, I would be tormented and tantalized by the strangest imaginings, really quite inappropriate in an anything-goes, come-and-get-me, wish-fulfilment scenario.

Instance. I dream that I am going down on a woman, giving her oral pleasure, underneath the sheets. All well and good. And, judging by the rhythmic movements of her pelvis, by her wetness and her eventual shuddering, she is very much enjoying herself. Top marks. Yet, when I come up for air, back into the light, I find her face is black and blue, her lip split, her nose broken, and her face smeared with fresh blood. As you can imagine, I am far from being pleased with the result of my labours.

Was the woman dead? I do not know. Was it I who injured her? I cannot tell. Is this imagining more real than what I imagine to have happened last time I performed cunnilingus in the waking world? I do not know that either.

Many people dream of being rock singers, film stars, or sporting heroes; of owning fast cars, beautiful homes, and wardrobes full of expensive clothes. Others dream of three decent meals a day, a roof over their head, basic sanitation, an education for their children, and a society in which they are safe from violence and oppression. In both cases, most will be gravely disappointed. Nevertheless, sanity demands that these people should regard their dreams as a model or prototype of a state of affairs which they hope to bring about in the real world. For to prefer muck to manna merely on the grounds of availability is lunacy indeed. But what about people who only have bad dreams? What does sanity demand of them?

(the undiscovered country from whose bourne no traveller returns — when to go, how to get there, prices and availability)

If you are at all sensitive to the sight of suffering, there is no doubt whatever that in the course of your travels you will see many things to appal you: wild animals dying slowly of disease, or being torn limb from limb by predators; malnourished and mistreated domestic animals; malnourished, mistreated, diseased, humiliated, bored, ill-educated, oppressed, over-worked, impoverished, unloved human beings of every age, every sex, every creed, every pigmentation imaginable.

Is there too much suffering in the world? Or is there exactly the right amount? I do not know. Neither do I know how one sets about discovering the answer to such a question.

It often seemed to me, as I was lounging on my Le Corbusier chaise, gazing lazily through the wall-to-wall, floor-to-ceiling windows of my genuine loft-style apartment, that there was a loud scream somewhere in the room. I could never tell whose scream it was. Indeed, it was so muted – swaddled perhaps in cotton wool and other materials of a sound-dampening nature – that I could not even hear it, let alone recognize the voice. Sometimes I would wander around the room, checking in cupboards and drawers, looking high and low for a big, sound-proofed box. I never found anything. Nevertheless, I felt certain that it was there, ululating insatiably, like an abandoned infant's cry. Perhaps the voice was mine, who knows? Anyway, the sensation always passed away soon enough, and I'd be left feeling as cheerful as before.

If you found such a box, would you open it? Would you pour soothing lotion on the blistered, reddened larynx within? Or would you leave it where it was, perhaps winding a little extra wadding around it, in case it grew louder during the night? Is there too much suffering in the world, or is there exactly the right amount?

Happening inadvertently upon a war-zone, for instance, you may witness at first hand the sight of lovelorn children wandering through the ruined streets in rags, hardly daring to seek home, hardly daring even to mention it, for fear that by craving it openly – they will scare it away again, scare it away for good. What are you to make of this spectacle?

I don't know. However, when contemplating the

leprous, the tuberculous, the HIV-infected, the hungry, etcetera etcetera etcetera, of this world, should you find yourself about to drown in unwanted feelings of pity and guilt, the following sophism might come in useful. Fact: far fewer people commit suicide in poverty-stricken, war-torn, disease-ravaged societies than in the comfy, economically advantaged West. Explanation: when faced with infinite toil, infinite grief, infinite fear, and infinite suffering, human beings are simply too preoccupied to stop and listen to the demons within. And it is only when the demons *are* within that self-slaughter becomes an attractive option. For suicide is a kind – a rather drastic kind – of exorcism, is it not? Yes, the one luxury affluent folk like you and I cannot afford is the luxury of that universal analgesic: adversity. And so it is that when, from time to time, I become aware of the suffering of the hapless hordes who inhabit this agonizing ball of pain we call planet Earth, I do not worry that my sufferings cannot possibly equal theirs. No, I rather feel envious of these people who have so much on their plates already that they have no need to spend their time wrestling with phantoms.

And so my advice to the conscience-stricken independent traveller is to emulate disadvantaged people everywhere: stay busy, load your wagon higher, clutch eagerly at straws, and keep moving. Do not, whatever you do, succumb to the temptation to feel guilty. But if you do succumb, try not to feel guilty about having done so. Go easy on yourself. Give yourself a break. A change is as good as a rest. If you have suffered an eating disorder in the past, next time why not try depression instead? If you've been depressed, try going for a psychotic breakdown. If paranoid psychosis has lost its charms, why not experiment with obsessive-compulsive behaviour?

Be creative. Don't feel obliged to restrict yourself to the disorders you inherited from your parents. Be aware that the taxonomy of major and minor mental illnesses changes constantly, as polymorphously unhappy humans break new ground in their effort simultaneously to conceal and express their woes. Allow yourself the same liberty. If you can't come up with anything really original, try looking for inspiration in old textbooks. If you happen across a superannuated psychiatric disorder that appeals to you, give it a whirl. Try dropping everything, literally everything, and walking, walking, walking – not knowing where you are going or why – until you finally come to rest, hundreds of miles from your home.* Try anything.

Above all, don't let yourself get stuck in a rut. Treat

---

* An illness that was first classified in the nineteenth century but has since fallen into desuetude; in my view a choice disorder which is ripe for a major revival.

life as if it were an experiment.* Tell yourself it is not your fault. Tell yourself you are one of Prince Kropotkin's round pegs, deformed and partially crushed to fit a square hole. Blame on your boots the fault of your feet, for, even if they do not chafe, they are almost certainly guilty of something. And, if you are tempted to end it all, try to do it slowly, as I have always done, giving yourself ample opportunity to turn back, just in case the prospects you are leaving behind should suddenly come to seem more appealing than the emptiness that lies ahead.

---

*   Sadly, it is. The results have not yet been published.

(to Scotland,* for no clear reason)

After years of solitary living, I found myself feeling
slightly oppressed by the presence of my new employee,
who kept looking at me as if she wanted to ask me a
question, or as if she imagined I had something I wanted
to ask her – as if it was any of her business. And so,
finding myself unable to sleep for several nights in a
row, even with the assistance of quite considerable doses
of Temazepam, I decided to take the overnight train to
Inverness. The very name of this 'sleeper' service is
strongly suggestive of a restful night and, although it is
both slower and at the same time more expensive than
flying, since I had nothing in particular to do when I got
there, I was in no great hurry to arrive. And so the
prospect of being cosseted in my own private cubicle,

---

* 'A treeless, flowerless land formed out of the refuse of the universe.'
  John Wilkes, MP (1727–97).

swathed in fresh white linen, whilst being rocked to sleep by the gentle swaying of the train, seemed more than worth the extra time and cost.

Temazepam having lost its potency for me in all but the most lung-crushing doses, in accordance with the rules of my circuit-abuse system I chose to leave this particular drug behind. In fact, I left all my drugs behind. But in order to get into the spirit of the trip, and to ensure that I would, in one way or another, be able to enjoy a moment or two of unconsciousness before dawn, I took with me a bottle of sixteen-year-old Lagavulin, a mild but flavoursome West Coast malt.

Packed the smallest of overnight bags (I had booked my return for the following evening), taking only the said whisky, a toothbrush, my shaving kit (comprising badger-hair shaving brush, shaving soap, cut-throat razor and strop), and a book. The book in question was *Robinson Crusoe* by Daniel Defoe. Do not ask me why.

My servant saw me off at the door. It was a touching scene. I rather think she should have had a couple of Labradors with her, or perhaps golden retrievers, which she could have struggled to hold by the collar or the scruff, as they scuffed at the floor in their eagerness to accompany me on my journey.

Snacked alone at the Ivy, just in case the in-train dining facilities should prove too dismal. Took a taxi to Euston Station and climbed aboard.

I had taken the precaution of buying a first-class ticket, so as to guarantee having a whole cabin to myself, and so that my night's rest would not be disturbed by some halitotic, conversationally challenged angler, off to the Spey for his annual fish-killing trip. Furthermore, I had fixed in my mind the wonderful train seduction sequence from *North by Northwest*, in which the roguish Cary Grant character, Roger O. Thornhill (is something R-O-Tten in the United States of America?) finally meets his duplicitous match in the laconic, lachrymose, kind-hearted spy-prostitute Eve 'a little trouty, but quite good' Kendal – played by the tail-waggingly spicy Eva Marie Saint.

Obviously I had not been mistaken for a fictional spy by enemy agents – and neither was I a mother-obsessed, dishonest, rakish ad-man who whenever he meets an attractive woman finds it necessary to start pretending he has no desire to make love to her – and so the hope of contriving some sort of replay of the scene, with myself in the male lead, was perhaps rather a vain one. Even so, there is a certain romance about train travel – especially when travelling through the night (through tunnels etcetera) – which was attractive to a young man like myself with a penchant for passionate encounters. And so a private cabin was a luxury that would, with luck, soon become an absolute necessity, should some Eva Marie Saint look-alike (or, better still, some Eve Kendal act-alike) happen my way.

My compartment was a little smaller than I had imagined, the linen a little less crisp, and the blankets somewhat more pilled. The wall-to-wall carpeting, of which the brochure had bragged somewhat intemperately, was a little more industrial than one had been led to believe. Even so, the motion of the train was restful and, when I had drunk approximately half my 75 cl bottle of *usquebaugh*,* I was feeling relaxed enough to explore the rest of the train.

The dining carriage was blandly comfortable rather than luxurious. The service was adequate but the menu, as I had expected, a little unadventurous. I ate a little duck with a half-bottle of Côtes du Rhône. Watching the world flash by was a pleasure: I never tire of a good blur, which is altogether different from a smear, a smudge, or, God forbid, a splotch – and a different thing again from a haunting crepuscular obscurity. For a blur is bright yet indistinct, and that makes all the difference. Many of my happiest experiences have been blurs.

There were people in the carriage, but no Eve; just businessmales and businessfemales, together with a smattering of that special type of foreigner who flies to London, garbs themselves in tweeds and waxed cotton, hooks a fly in their hatband, then travels up to Scotland

---

* Fr. Scots Gaelic *uisge beatha*, meaning 'water of life'. Traditionally a breakfast drink.

to strut around in shopping centres, nibbling shortbread from tartan wrappers, and wrinkling their noses up at oatcakes and whisky.

Obliged to cast my net further afield, I walked the length of the train. Second-class* was steaming with common humanity – in the sociological sense, you understand; I couldn't vouch for their kindness or warmth or solidarity with their co-existents. Coach G (second class) appeared at first to offer a possible harbour for the lonely traveller, until her boyfriend arrived back from the buffet car. I bought a packet of cigarettes from the buffet in order to have the excuse of sitting down in the smoking section, should I find someone I wished to smoke with. I did not.

Back in the dining car I picked at a little smoked salmon – nothing trouty about it – and drank a half-bottle of Pouilly Fumé. Amused myself for a while by solving the philosophical problem of solipsism.

Solipsism is the belief that *I* am the only person who has conscious experience, feels pain, etcetera. It is an interesting problem, and all the more pleasant to ponder because it has already been solved: Ludwig Wittgenstein proved very brilliantly that, as it is with monarchs, so it is with pains: if they exist at all then they must exist

---

* I don't know about you, but I find the modern habit of describing second-class as 'standard' depressing for all concerned.

publicly; for otherwise their titles would be meaningless and their authority unrecognized.

So you may rest assured: you do feel pain, I know you do. I may forget the fact now and then, but ultimately I do not doubt it. Yes, I know how much it hurts.

Growing increasingly bored,* as the sun went down and the fields and hedgerows and trees and towns and cows and calves turned first into shadows, then into simple darkness punctuated by lumps of light, I suddenly realized – or rather, I remembered – that I was in love with Tamora.† I have known Tamora for several years. A frail and delicate creature with long sharp claws, she and I have spent many a long lunch, and many a longer dinner, gazing across our wine glasses at each other, waiting to see who would be the first to break cover. We each carry a large supply of Cupid's darts whenever we meet, ready to plunge them deep into the other's heart the moment our long-running truce is breached. Made a note in my diary to pursue my affair with her *without restraint* the moment I set foot back in London.

Returned to my room, mixed the Lagavulin with a

---

* You and me both, no doubt.

† I often have such insights whilst travelling. The blurring effect breaks one's ties with the here and now, and facilitates deeper insight into one's soul.

splash of Scottish spring water, and necked the whole lot down from the bottle. Opened the window and rode for fifteen minutes with the upper half of my body steeping in the cool night air, which tore at my clothes and flowed over my skin like a river of balm. Threw my train ticket, cash, credit cards, driving licence, diary, wallet, and wristwatch out of the window just south of Glasgow, then retired to bed, to be rocked unconscious by the loving motion of the train.

(chapter 1)

It is a truth universally acknowledged, that a single man in possession of a good fortune, must be in want of a wife.

(here we go)

The steward very kindly woke me an hour and a half before our arrival in Inverness with a tray of addled eggs, slaughtered bacon, mistreated tomato, and something brown that I found difficult to characterize to my entire satisfaction, but which I'm fairly sure must have involved the desecration of what was once a potato. Slung the whole stinking mess back out into the corridor, just managing to clip the steward on the back of the neck with the tray. Slammed shut the door, vomited in the sink, then returned to bed for another hour of undisturbed slumber.

While I was sleeping, my grandmother came into the cabin. Smiling warmly, she asked me why I had not visited her lately. I found this confusing, since I knew for a fact that she had been dead for at least ten years. On reflection, however, I realized that this was just another example of the ingrained selfishness of old people who, given half a chance, would suck the blood from those like myself who are young, fit, and full of life.

Disembarked at Inverness, which I had always believed to be somewhere north of London, but which must have somehow slipped into the Southern Hemisphere, for it was midwinter there. Found a copy of the *Financial Times* in a rubbish bin, wrapped myself in it, and snuggled down on a bench to read the preface to *Robinson Crusoe*.

> If ever the story of any private man's adventures in the world were worth making public, and were acceptable when published, the editor of this account thinks this will be so.
>
> The wonders of this man's life exceed all that (he thinks) is to be found extant; the life of one man being scarce capable of a greater variety.
>
> The story is told with modesty, with seriousness, and with a religious application of events to the uses to which wise men always apply them (viz.) to the instruction of others by this example, and to justify and honour the wisdom of Providence in all the variety of our circumstance, let them happen how they will.

My powers of concentration spent, I fell asleep.

(strange meeting)

Awoke in a state of some confusion, which could only be explained in terms of a dawning condition of sobriety. Staggering around on the platform like something that has just been born, or is about to die – only time can solve such conundrums – I found myself approached by a friendly, wizened Glaswegian man named Terry, who asked me if I had a few moments to spare. Reluctantly I admitted that I did.

We sit down together, and Terry tells me the good news, which is that I am loved by a Jewish man from somewhere in the Middle East, who has been dead for considerably longer than my grandma. I can't see how this news can possibly be of any interest or benefit to me, and tell my evangelist so. Terry informs me that I must understand that this dead Jewish man is the Lord – *my* Lord, in fact – and that he died so that I could have eternal life. This annoys me because, if it is true, it amounts to the most astonishing imposition, really no better than one of those offers of cut-price weekend breaks that credit-card companies use in an attempt to lure you into some ill-advised contract for insurance, or whatever; I don't want the holiday, I don't want the insurance, I don't want my waste-basket cluttered up with your junk mail, so fuck off.

I explain my objections to Terry, who drones on irrelevantly about blessings and other necromantic fantasies. Eventually I ask him how on earth he manages to make a living from attempting to co-opt complete strangers into his bizarre, fetishistic religious practices, and he confesses to me, smirking somewhat as he does so, that he lives on state handouts. I tell him that if he doesn't go away immediately I will report him to the Department of Social Security. He tells me that I am damned. I concur willingly, and he leaves me in peace.

My mobile phone, which I forgot to dispense with on the train, rings. I see from the display that it is Tamora, of all people, who is attempting to get in touch. I know for a fact that Tamora hates me, because I once tried to have sexual intercourse with her but could not get it up – probably because I know her for the shallow, selfish, grasping bitch she undoubtedly is. I turn the phone off, wrap it in the Companies and Markets section of the *FT*, and deposit it in a rubbish bin.

In the public lavatory I meet a man called David, who

really does seem to love me. That is to say, he offers to let me fuck him in the mouth, or in the arse (with a condom, which he can supply), entirely free of charge, and with no obligation to provide reciprocal services. I know love when I see it, and I'm pretty sure that this must be it. David is a well-built, good-looking young man who, although he is wearing a football scarf, seems none the less sensitive and likeable for that. I forgive him for being a football supporter, reasoning that he is probably too badly educated to realize the folly of standing in a large crowd, barking and howling at a ball like a brain-damaged dog.

I am wondering whether and if so how to extricate myself from his (I think) genuinely kind, yet equally genuinely unwanted advances, without causing undue offence, when a compelling gastric necessity forces me to rush into one of the cubicles. David mistakes my sudden dash for an erotoleptic fit and follows me in. Spurred on by the divine madness of eros, I get down on my knees and attempt to throw up in the toilet bowl, while David – who is perhaps feeling sick – reaches round and struggles to get my cock out of my trousers.

There are few things less satisfying than attempting to vomit when nothing remains in the stomach to be disgorged (unless, perhaps, it is attempting to cry when the heart is devoid of grief and the lachrymal sacs parched of tears) – and having someone trying to stick their fingers up your arse while you are fighting the good fight adds little to overall levels of enjoyment.

Struggling, between dry retches, to explain to David that I am not fully convinced that he is the man for me, I find my diplomatic skills hampered by sheer physical incapacity: I can neither express dissent nor cooperate. My would-be lover seems to take my lack of enthusiasm very personally indeed, and begins beating me around the torso with his fists and feet, paying particular attention to the kidneys. The football scarf was perhaps a red herring, for it is clear now that David specializes in contact sports.

Relieved as ever to find myself used according to my desert, my nausea passes away and I struggle to my feet under a welter of blows. We wrestle for a while, until I finally succeed in unlocking the cubicle door. Unable to dislodge my beau from his position as gatekeeper, I am eventually forced to simulate carnal enthusiasm, embracing him and giving him a big, bilious kiss on the lips. When I feel his body relax against mine I twirl him around, tango-style, and throw him against the back wall of the cubicle. He trips and bangs his head on the cistern, which stuns him for just long enough to allow me to open the door and (I will say it now) pronk out of the lavatory building, hobbled as I am by my trousers and underpants, which are tangled tightly around my ankles.

Presbyterian eyebrows are raised, but I recover my decency in a few moments, and no one shows any sign of attempting to effect a citizen's arrest; nor does anyone, so far as I can tell, attempt to call the police. Even so, I hot-foot it out of the railway station and into the streets of Inverness.

It is a gloriously overcast day, with a strong hint of drizzle to come, and a chill, cheerful north-easterly wind, which seems to bear upon it a vile odour of fermented fish, carried across the North Sea no doubt from Trondheim.* Walking fast in no particular direction, I take deep breaths and check my face for signs of bleeding. As far as I can tell, my visage is intact. So no improvement there, then.

---

* There are only three things to do in Trondheim: drinking, fucking, and fishing – and in the winter there is no fishing. Altogether an ideal place to spend the dark months.

(a long, hot winter)

Finding myself – physically speaking – beside the peat-stained waters of the river Ness, I drape myself over the railings, which presumably are there to prevent water-sports enthusiasts from inadvertently flinging themselves into the torrent, and consider my next move. The steep grassy bank is covered with daffodils, which are, I remember, edible. Feeling the need for something to settle my stomach, I slither underneath the bottom railing and ensconce myself amongst the blooms, which I nibble at happily, a petal here, a bell there. So as not to be accused of illegally picking flowers, I do not use my hands, but remain on hands and knees, browsing like a ruminant. Some of the daffodils are actually narcissi, which have a certain piquancy about them, a hint of something peppery, perhaps. I consume them with great pleasure.

A pleasant Japanese couple – whom I suspect but

cannot be sure are the same two who recorded my Trafalgar Square perigee – take several photographs of me. I wave and smile for the camera, and the tourists seem highly gratified. Shortly afterwards, my hunger sated, I am kneeling by the gurgling waters of the Ness, brushing my teeth (I hope you did not imagine I would ever throw my washbag away), when two policemen arrive and coax me on to the pavement with the offer of a little chat. I have never been one to refuse an offer of polite conversation, and conform with their wishes with something approaching alacrity.

With great patience I explain to them that the breakfast on the sleeper from London was far from satisfactory; but this information seems rather to increase their condition of perplexity than to relieve it. One of them suggests that I had better take the matter up with the railway operator. I thank him for his advice, but assure him that I have already made my feelings clear on that score.

More inconsequential chit-chat follows, culminating in an invitation for me to accompany them to the police station, where further enquiries might be made. I wonder aloud whether I am under arrest. The two functionaries exchange glances, wander off, confer, return, ask me for my name, then radio their station sergeant for advice as to what, if anything, they might charge me with. I take the opportunity provided by their lengthy deliberations to clip my toenails, in preparation for the long journey ahead. The policemen return from their vehicle a few moments later to inform me that I am not under arrest on this occasion, but that I should consider myself cautioned vis-à-vis further encroachments against the flora and fauna of the fair town of Inverness, capital of the Highlands.

I bid my uniformed super egos good-day and proceed directly to a nearby supplier of outdoor goods, where I select a functional, lightweight yet waterproof pair of hiking boots, a good set of breathable outer garments, a sturdy pair of gaiters, a head-mounted torch (with spare batteries), a compass, a Swiss army knife, a one-litre water bottle, and a small but comfortable rucksack,* into which I transfer my copy of *Robinson Crusoe* and my washbag, ostensibly in order to test out the rucksack's weight-bearing capacities. Sending the shop assistant into the back of the shop by means of a specious enquiry regarding the possibility of fitting crampons to my tennis shoes, I hike out of the shop in full backwoods regalia, then sprint across the road and dodge into a convenient alleyway. I attract very little attention from passers-by, once I switch off my head-mounted torch.

Making my way back towards the river, I check into

---

* Which promises to redistribute the load from my back to my hips. And why not?

a comfortable-looking hotel under the – I thought – rather witty pseudonym Laurens Van der Post. Take a room overlooking the river. Eat a good meal of Cumberland sausage, mashed potatoes and boiled peas, followed by another equally good meal of Cumberland sausage, mashed potatoes and boiled peas, followed by a third portion of Cumberland sausage, mashed potatoes and boiled peas, which sadly I am unable to consume in its entirety. Then I retire to bed.

Sleep soundly until midnight.

(thought for the night)

If God existed, it would be necessary to destroy him.

(early start)

On waking, set about fortifying myself by consuming the entire contents of the mini-bar, drinking everything with an interesting flavour first, then consuming the chocolate snacks – which as you know put the taste buds out of action and render any effort to enjoy even a moderately fine wine or malt whisky nugatory – before finally polishing off the cheap vodka, gin, tinned lager, etcetera. Filled my water bottle and left the hotel at around two o'clock in the morning, stealing a postcard from reception on my way out. The card bore a photo of the River Ness, together with the stunningly apposite legend 'Greetings from Inverness'. Adorned the reverse with the following verse:

> *Mother, may I go and bathe?*
> *Yes, my darling daughter.*
> *Hang your clothes on yonder tree*
> *But don't go near the water.*

Addressed the card to Aphro and posted it, without a stamp. Proceeded to a 24-hour-garage, where I stole a four-miles-to-one-inch map of Great Britain.*

Took a minicab along the south side of Loch Ness on the B852. Loch Ness is the largest volume of fresh water in Great Britain, reaching a depth of 788 feet (240 m) and a length of about 23 miles (36 km). It lies in the Great Glen (Glen More nan Albin) that runs from north-east to south-west, bisecting the Highlands, and forms part of the system of waterways which Thomas Telford (the great Scottish civil engineer) opened to navigation by means of the Caledonian Canal (completed 1822), thus providing a passageway between Atlantic ocean and the North Sea.

Loch Ness's watershed extends to more than 700 square miles (1,800 square km), the loch itself being fed by several rivers, including the Oich and the Enrick. Its outlet is the River Ness (see above), which flows into the Moray Firth. Seiches (surface oscillations), caused by differential heating, are common on the loch. The water level rises and falls sharply throughout the year, which is one reason for the loch's scanty flora. Another is the great depth of water near the shoreline. Abyssal fauna is also sparse.

Like some other very deep lochs in Scotland and

---

* As it is humorously known by the inmates.

Scandinavia, Loch Ness is said to be inhabited by an aquatic monster. Many sightings of the so-called Loch Ness monster have been reported, and the possibility of its existence – perhaps in the form of a solitary survivor from the long-extinct genus of aquatic reptiles *plesiosaurus* – continues to intrigue many people.*

Growing increasingly fascinated by the deep, dark waters of that great tectonic meeting place, I stopped my driver just south-west of Dores, ostensibly in order to have a look for the sorrowful, solitary plesiosaur of our dreams, who moans quietly to himself, out of time and out of place, in deep cold water. Stepped gently from the vehicle, then went running off into a nearby wood, hooting and screaming.†

When the driver had given up looking for me, I back-tracked to Dores and took the B862 southbound towards Torness. Reached the junction with the B851 in good time. Switched on my head-torch and left the road, heading due south – a compass course of (approximately) 185° 30′.

Scotland is rich in animal life. Herds of red deer graze in the corries and remote glens. Although formerly a

---

* Sad, but true. Look into thine own abyssal depths, Oh enthusiasts, and you might find what you're searching for.
† A wholly philanthropic gesture: since my driver was not going to receive fair remuneration for his labours, the least I could do was provide him with an amusing story to tell his friends.

woodland species, they are now found mainly on higher ground, but roe deer still inhabit the woods, along with sika and fallow deer (both exotic species). Foxes and badgers are widespread, and the number of wildcats is thought to be increasing.* Other resident mammals include the pine marten, the otter, the mountain hare and the brown hare. A handful of ospreys nest in Scotland, together with golden eagles, buzzards, peregrine falcons, and kestrels. The red grouse – the Scottish subspecies of the willow grouse – is gunned down on sight, for pleasure and nutrition. Buzzards and golden eagles are gunned down by gamekeepers because they hunt game birds too. Other species of grouse include the capercaillie and the ptarmigan, which is found only at higher altitudes and turns snow-white in winter.

But it was dark, and I could see none of these things. Indeed, I could see very little indeed, save the heather and the grass directly in front of my feet, and perhaps a little bog cotton. The sky was overcast and no moon shone.

Scotland has a temperate, maritime climate, milder than might be expected for its latitude, with considerable local variations. Rainfall is greatest in the mountainous areas of the west, as the prevailing south-westerly winds

---

* Sadly, however, they've taken to mating with domestics, imperilling both their future as a species and their reputation for good taste.

come laden with moisture from the Atlantic. East winds are common only in winter and spring, when cold, dry continental air masses envelop the North Sea. Hence the west tends to be milder in winter, but in summer damper and cloudier than the east. Tiree, in the Inner Hebrides, has a mean temperature in winter of 41° F (5° C) in the coldest month (the same as the south-east of England), whereas Dundee, on the east coast, has 37° F (2.8° C). Conversely, Dundee's mean temperature in the warmest month is 59° F (15° C) and Tiree's 57° F (13.9° C).

Rainfall varies remarkably. Some two-thirds of Scotland exceeds Britain's annual average of 40 inches (1,000 millimetres) annually, with a staggering 142 inches in the Ben Nevis area. In the flat Outer Hebrides, rainfall is lower, as are annual averages in the east – the Moray Firth (Inverness) having less than 25 inches. In winter, a significant amount of snow falls above 1,500 feet throughout the Highlands.

On the night in question it was fucking cold, for the unseasonable north-easterly I described earlier in my diatribe was still blowing strong. The smell of rotting fish from Scandinavia had, however, subsided. Instead, a dreary mizzle cascaded slowly, slowly, slowly against the outer surfaces of my soul; a process which reminded me of the obsessive way archaeologists have of spraying water on those ancient ships they retrieve from the mud, so as to keep them thoroughly hydrated while they prepare their preservative potions, lest their antediluvian novelty should otherwise desiccate, and crumble into dust.

When the sun came up I made a very comfortable bed of heather and lay down under a rock, shivering violently and praying for death to come along and stick something in me. Perhaps I was thinking of David?

(the Monadhliath mountains)

The *Monadh Liath* – or Grey Hills – form an extensive, undulating plateau to the north-west of the Spey Valley. Lower than the Cairngorms, which lie to the east, and the Mamores, which lie to the south-west, the Monadhliath have fewer ridges and glaciated corries than these ranges, and present a profile that is generally smoother and more rounded. Even so, there are several summits above 3,000 ft (900 m), the highest being Carn Liath – the Grey Hill itself – at 1,006 m. Eagles and wildcats make their homes in the Monadhliath. But then, they don't have much choice in the matter: if they lived anywhere less barren, human beings would destroy them. It's an abominably cold and lonely place, even in May; I'd recommend taking a taxi down the A9 and missing it out altogether.

Awoke with the sun high in the sky. The thick gray turf of cloud had been rolled away and the wind had

251

dropped to the merest cat's-paw. Pennants of nacreous cirrus formed an iridescent lip around the sun, while perky clumps of fair-weather cumulus performed their slow-motion celestial tumbling act. Together, these atmospheric effects suggested an emotion that was perhaps somewhat akin to joy, I wouldn't know. My arms were numb from hugging myself against the cold, and my legs were numb for some other reason – or, what is more likely, for no reason at all, for my body is wilful. I rolled out from under my rock and into the healing rays of our humble star. Stared at a piece of golden-gray grass six inches from my eyes. It impressed me so much – or I stared at it so hard – that I eventually could not distinguish between that piece of grass and myself. All the better.

Feeling melodramatically inclined, I fell asleep muttering the couplet:

> *If anything might rouse him now,*
> *The kind old sun will know.*

It did not rouse me; at least, it did not do so quickly. For I stayed where I was, sleeping and waking, sleeping and waking, until the sun was nudging against the horizon, begging entry to the night. When I did sleep I dreamed that I was lying on a barren moor, lonely and afraid, with sunlight pouring through me like water through a sieve. When I awoke, I found myself lying on a barren moor, lonely and afraid, with sunlight pouring through me like water through a sieve. Who says there is no truth in dreams?

I moved, eventually, probably through sheer inertia; for I have been moving aimlessly to and fro for as long as I can remember. When I raised my head from the heather I found that I was very close to a herd of what must have been red deer – mangy, grubby gray creatures with a fugitive look in their eyes. They had plenty of friends, despite their uncouth appearance, for there must have been sixty of them in all. I felt painfully hungry. Lying very still, I scrabbled around for a suitable stone, which I eventually located and prised out of the peat with my fingernails.

The nearest deer was about twenty-five feet away. It was a tired old stag. I stood up and hurled myself towards it. I made good ground at first, but the deer made better and, unfortunately, after about ten paces, I fell flat on my face in a peat bog, before even having had chance to hurl my rock. I hurled it anyway, for practice, once I had extricated myself from the sucking black mire. Then I took out my Swiss Army knife and brandished it at the deer – now approximately half a mile away from me – so as to let them know who was boss.

Revived by my exertions, I staggered on. I had

trudged for perhaps an hour before it crossed my mind to wonder where I was going. That was when I discovered I had lost my compass. Keeping the sun to my right, I barely flinched at my misfortune, but pressed onwards, thinking of food. As the sky reddened I forgot about food and concentrated on fearing the imminent onset of night. The absence of significant cloud cover meant that the earth would cool quickly. My bones were aching and my head felt curiously hollow. I found myself grinding my teeth together incessantly, and sucking on my tongue, and drinking far more water than seemed good for me.

The harder I marched, however, the less painful these symptoms became. I wondered whether I was strong enough to walk until dawn, when the sun might rise again. I somehow doubted it. But to collapse outright might bring satisfactions of its own, when compared to cowering beneath a rock, or in a cave, or out in the open, nurturing my last ounce of energy. Yes, I concluded: to collapse outright was the way ahead.

The moon rose. I marched to its rhythm. *I see the moon, the moon sees me, the moon sees somebody I want to see.* Still no substantive thoughts in my head; just pains and weakness and ineffective strategies for eluding them. Not really thinking about which way I was heading, but seemingly very certain about which way to turn,

I began to wonder if some kind of instinct might at last have taken over. The idea excited me.

I didn't collapse. I was a little disappointed not to; there is something curiously enticing about the notion of reaching the limits of one's endurance – and therefore, I suppose, the limit of oneself, with all the spurious promise of liberation that impossibility entails. But without the use of narcotics this feat seems peculiarly difficult to achieve. Instead I scrambled on through the heather, tripping regularly, often narrowly avoiding injuring myself on the boulders and sharp rocks that lurked beneath the soft, springy surface. I developed the habit of taking a dive the moment I put a foot slightly wrong; a good technique, which I believe could be adapted for use in other circumstances.

It was a relief to climb higher, where the heather was shallower, and eventually did not grow at all. The extra exertion involved in going uphill helped concentrate the pain into my thighs and lungs, and being surrounded on every side by steep escarpments was exhilarating. Is exhilarating the word? Perhaps comforting is a better; sharp drops are comforting, for they hold the promise of sudden extinguishment.

I broached a summit – an undulating plateau covered in grit and shards of rock and tiny plants. The views were unholy: I could have been nowhere; I could have been in a dream. I could have been perched on the roughened face of a tiny planet, spinning out of control through space. Emptiness, macrocosmic and microcosmic, prevailed.

I felt bad tempered as I descended, for I knew that sooner or later I would have to ascend again. And perhaps I had been enjoying the ghastly panoramic void. Disturbed what must have been a hare – a kind of rabbit with balls. It went scooting off across the rocks, clattering cleverly. Stood still, watching, as it raced down the denuded mountainside. It was pleasant to have company.

Slipped down a scree and hit my face on a boulder. The bang to my head threatened to wake me, into what other world I do not know. But the pain subsided and I did not succumb. The flesh around my eye was cut, and blood dripped into my mouth. I found the flavour curiously satisfying. It is heartening to be reminded that one contains such wholesome, such universal human stuff. I wondered about making a pudding out of it, but the flow stopped before I could fathom a way of harvesting it.

I staggered on, dreaming of sleep, dreaming of the sun, aiming for the next peak. In the valley the heather tugged furiously at my ankles, bringing me down time and time again. Once or twice I seemed unlikely to get up. Heady moments. Once I fell asleep, and found myself dreaming of a time when I was young, and had shared a hotel room with my sister: we had played together, fighting and scratching, loving each other. I stood up, disgusted by the sentimental turn my thoughts had taken, and forced myself onwards.

Dawn broke shortly afterwards. The Scottish dawn is a sustained dawn, during the summer months. It is the same in all the northern latitudes; when the sun finally emerges you are sick of it.

I fell down by a stream and slept fitfully, eventually putting my rucksack over my head to keep out the light. The morning seemed mild, but I felt too hot and too cold by turns, and was kept awake by fits of shivering and sweating. My legs were stiff with exertion, and an indescribably vague and horrible pain – an icy conflagration – consumed my flesh. Even after I had been lying still for several hours, I remained short of breath. The sound of the stream rang and rumbled in my dreams like an ecstatic emergency bell – an uncanny alarm which signified nothing beyond the catastrophe of its own ringing.

By midday the sun had grown hot and for the first time since starting out I took off my weatherproof shell, you know what I mean. The sky was blue to a fault and there was no wind, so I also took off the jacket of my Giorgio Armani suit. It had taken a bit of a battering – white sweat stains under the arms and crotch. Eventually

I took off all my clothes and washed in the stream. The cold water set my heart palpitating violently, as my body convulsed and shuddered. I went through with it even so, washing the salt from surface and corner alike. My flesh was all goose bumps, which felt good.

I, on the other hand, felt dreadfully faint and dizzy, for the water roused my senses and reminded my body that it was being starved. I lay down naked on the heather, shivering uncontrollably. But when I put my shirt and suit back on I immediately felt too hot. Plumping for heat over cold – for the heat was merely uncomfortable, while the cold made my whole body vibrate – I kept my suit on, put my head inside my rucksack, and slept.

Woke up screaming and sobbing. Hugged myself in an effort to calm myself down, but I cannot have found this show of affection sincere, for the screaming and sobbing continued. Infinitely small speck in infinite space growing infinitely smaller at an infinite rate. Screaming no good then. Calmed myself. Calm no good either. Screamed again. Screaming not so bad second time round.* Continued screaming for several minutes. Eventually stood up, the bag still in place over my head, and threw myself forcibly to the ground. Banged my knee. Yelped like a dog. Felt . . . subdued. Excruciating

---

* Improved technique?

pain always does the trick. Tried for another sob, but nothing doing.

It was cold. I was cold. I was it.

It replaced its waterproof suit and started moving, walking directly towards the sun, that it might warm itself in the wholesome rays. When it was warmed through – more as a result of exertion than solar radiation, for the sun was by now low in the sky and shone but weakly, though prettily enough – it turned away, leaving the sun to its right, in order that it might be moving broadly southwards, so that one day it might reach civilization or, what is perhaps not the same thing, home.

The moon was high and full and white as an old bone. I did not march to its rhythm; I staggered, rather, and stumbled, and occasionally rolled. Slipped and scudded down a hillside into a broad-bottomed valley. In the distance a row of peaks. Trudged towards. Faint with weakness. Felt it only faintly. Pale blue sky behind the black and tumble of the stars. Felt very little. Seemed to be going deaf. A screaming fit petered out for want of an audience. Punched myself in the face, for pride.

Climbed, climbed, climbed.

Skidded down a scree and fell off a cliff. Fell through spinning space. Stars were out in force, whispering of love unknown. Landed in the heather, winded but unharmed. A cracked rib, perhaps, nothing more.

Seemed unfair in the circumstances. Scrambled to my feet, returned to the path, and climbed, bitterly bitter. Taste in my mouth. Had forgotten to clean my teeth. Had forgotten to bring food. Not even a sheep to gnaw on.

Breezy on summit. Could see . . . a valley with a road, running by a loch. Lay down and shivered on the dewy grass before beginning the descent. Headed east across the plateau, to the top of Puist Coire Ardair (1,070 m), then along the narrower ridge with good views on the left down into Coire Ardair. Bore east-north-east across the flat-topped dome of Sron a'Choire (1,001 m) before descending eastwards down a wide, shallow corrie towards Aberarder. Crossed the Allt Coire Ardair by means of the footbridge to the west of the farm. Made a devil of a row at the farm, doing the best impression I could muster of a suppliant Odysseus, imploring, beseeching and entreating until I was (dark) blue in the face. Eventually succeeded in convincing the residents (though not myself) that I was to be pitied rather than feared. They let me in and gave me some soup.

Vomited, took two paracetamol, and resumed my journey.

(the continuation)

Around thirty-five miles to the south-west of Creag Meagaidh (which mountain I had just as it were *conquered*), lies Ben Nevis (the Venomous Hill), the highest peak in the British Isles. Ben Nevis is notable both for the fine arête connecting it to the adjoining Carn Mor Dearg (the Big Red Hill), and for its north-eastern face, which presents what is perhaps the most sublime array of cliffs of any mountain in Scotland. Certain nooks and crannies retain snow throughout the summer months, and in these places conditions of permafrost are almost present. It consists of a superstructure of volcanic rocks raised above the ancient schists of the Highlands. Directly to the south of this colossus, between Loch Leven and Glen Nevis, lies one of the finest mountain ranges in Scotland, the Mamores – a fine, glacier-scalloped ridge that runs from east to west, forming a formidable natural barrier to human traffic.

In order to attack the Venomous Hill by its inaccessible north-eastern face – the ascent of which I was definitively ill-equipped to attempt, both physically and psychologically – I would first of all have to trek some thirty miles or so along the relatively salubrious Glen Spean. To mitigate the unappealing clemency of this route, I decided to follow the A86 west along the north bank of Loch Laggan, leave the road at Moy Lodge, head south for half an hour, before resuming my policy of walking as a crow is supposed to fly, or a bee, towards its nest or hive, respectively. This would oblige me to swim across the bitterly cold Loch Treig, then ascend several estimable mountain peaks, before finally and conclusively destroying myself on the way up the Ben.

Fatigued, ravenously hungry, and increasingly unwell as a consequence of continuous exposure to the elements, which do not agree with me – but none the less pleased with my new plan, which seemed likely to bring me some kind of satisfaction at last – I fell down in a ditch and slept like a lover.

(the keeper of nothingness)

I was awoken by Dawn, who had wrapped her rosy
fingers around my cock and was tugging furiously. I was
very much hoping that she might embrace my petulant
member between her even rosier lips, or even enfold it
amidst the lush membranes of her ruby-coloured cunt,
when I became aware that I was lying penis down in
a ditch, hipping it. I was fatigued, ravenously hungry,
and increasingly unwell as a consequence of continuous exposure to the elements, which, I say it a second
time, do not agree with me. But I will not say that sleep
had brought me no benefits. No, I was a fraction less
delirious than I had been a few hours earlier, and now
realized that my new plan was a very stupid one, unlikely
to bring me any kind of satisfaction at all.

To recapitulate a point I have already made in a
previous chapter, decapitation is *not* the best cure for
toothache. That is to say, as a rule of thumb, suicide

should only be attempted by people who are very, very happy;* for only in a state of unalloyed ecstasy are we capable of making reliable judgements on such vexed questions as whether or not life is worth living, is a snare and a burden, has (or needs) a meaning, etcetera. Everyone else should wait and see what transpires. On this particular occasion, I was feeling only *moderately* glad to be alive, so prudence dictated that I should continue my trek southwards by a less perilous route.

I hobbled along the A82. All around me, birds were singing their little odes to joy, their music echoing across the still waters of Loch Laggan. One wonders what human conversation must sound like to them: a kind of pained and irregular groaning, perhaps, such as a ship's mast makes in high winds. A buzzard came along, but the little birds ganged up and chased it away.

As the sun began climbing the southern sky I felt almost certain that something would very shortly be revealed to me. I have felt this before; nothing ever is. I walked along the road for fifteen miles. It wasn't long before the pain from my aching feet and tired legs began to dominate my world. Perhaps that was the revelation I had been waiting for. If so, it was nothing new to me. It

---

* Cases where self-slaughter is the only feasible way of defending oneself against the unwanted attentions of the medical profession excepted.

hurt, I kept on walking; it hurt a little more, I walked a little faster. Eventually I couldn't bear the monotony any longer and turned off the road. I forded the River Spean without bothering to take off my boots. The cold, clear water brought temporary relief to my sores. I stood in the middle for a while, staring at the current, dreaming vaguely of baptism. Could water, without more, possibly be enough? I had taken enough showers in the past. But in the shower I had always used soap; what I needed was a little ritual.

Eventually the cold drove me to the bank, where I stumbled on through the heather, across a great open plain with mountains beyond. Finally, I began to fade. This is it, I thought to myself. I have reached the end of my evasions.

Just before noon I fell down in the heather, my heart pounding against my ribs like a lunatic hammering on the bars of his cell. *Let me out, let me out*, it cried. *You have nowhere to go*, I replied. Exhaustion crawled across the surface of my skin like an infestation. My muscles were spent. Blood, and very little else, was pulsing in my brain. My skeleton felt ready and willing to be stripped of this all too human flesh, felt ready to declare itself, to stand forth as the prevaricating grave-fodder it was.

I existed, I ceased to exist for a while, then I existed again. The sky too was undecided, gray here, blue there, white in another place. A slight breeze got up and I began to shiver uncontrollably. The shivering seemed somehow irrelevant, but there was nothing I could do to check it.

I could die here, I said to myself. I could just die, through no fault of my own. Everything I've always wanted, both at the same time. I waited, but it didn't seem to be happening.

Then the air changed. I sat up and looked around me.

At first I thought it was a hallucination – but no. In the distance, marching towards me, a rifle slung across both shoulders, his arms hooked over either end like a rambling crucifixion, was a tweed-clad stalker. I remained seated as he approached, a good-natured smile already visible on his weatherworn face.

'You're taking a rest in the heather, I see,' the man said to me. It's funny when people talk to you like that, telling you something about yourself quite out of the blue, something that you probably already knew and may well not have wanted to be reminded of; it gives a person an appearance of percipience which more often than not is wholly undeserved. One always imagines they will go on to tell you something about your history, filling in those little gaps for you, explaining how you made it home after such and such a party for instance, and how you came to have so much cake in the pockets of your coat. And perhaps those bigger gaps too, such as where you've been for the last twenty-five years, and why you bothered . . . faking it. They never do, though. The truth is, they talk like that just to let you know that you're there. Sweet, really.

'Can I have a look at that gun?' I asked the man without further ado.

'Aye, surely,' he answered, pleased that I was taking an interest.

'Is it loaded?' I asked him as I hoisted myself to my feet.

'No, no, you'll be fine.'

I took the weapon from him and weighed it in my hands, exploring its contours, its freshly anointed barrel, its well-polished stock.

'Where do the bullets go?' I asked him, knowing the answer full well. He showed me. 'Do they really fit in that tiny hole?' I asked. 'I would have thought they'd have to be bigger than that to bring down a full-grown stag.'

'No, no,' he explained. 'Look here.' He took a bullet from his leather pouch and showed me how it fitted. 'That'll do the job for you, so long as you get him through the head.' He slipped in a bullet and pushed the bolt home. We stood facing one another, each with both our hands upon the gun, admiring its potential energy.

'I see,' I mused.

The man was wiry, a little shorter than myself, but fit

and strong-looking. I felt a tension rising in my limbs. I wasn't sure whether it was strength or weakness. Spittle was rising in my throat, and tears brimming in my eyes. I swallowed hard. The man noticed that something was not quite right. He was about to say something – something along the lines of, There's something not quite right, laddie – when I made my move.

I didn't like to do it to him, but there you go. Snatching the weapon from his hands I pushed him violently backwards and he toppled over in the heather. I stood there for a moment to see what he would do, out of interest more than anything else. He eyed me curiously, as if he had been half expecting such treatment and did not really mind it. He didn't appear to be making any plans, so I left him there and moved away from him, away towards the sun, which had just appeared, showman-like, from behind a curtain of cloud.

In emptiness and desolation, I took aim at my right foot. An awful silence was about to be ended. I heard a voice. It was the stalker. 'It's all right, laddie,' he was saying to me. I thought about it for a moment. He was probably right. Then I pulled the trigger.

The shot resounded and I fell to the ground.

That's what happens when you're standing on two feet and shoot yourself through one of them. It's simple physics, really.

(striding out)

In most primates the foot is adapted for grasping. In humans, it is the hand that fulfils that function,* while our feet are adapted for a form of bipedalism known as the stride. *Australopithecus africanus*, who lived between two and five million years ago, had an entirely modern foot, and therefore probably strode.†

The repeated sequence in which the foot bears the body's weight is heel, lateral edge, ball, big toe. At the end of each stride the big toe transmits both weight and propulsive force. Unlike in other primates, this toe converges with the others and is held in place by strong

---

* In combination with that highly specialized, dimly lit part of the brain where liberal ideology holds sway.
† I can see him now, lurching anxiously through the sun-drenched bush, wondering which way, if any, is home.

ligaments. Its phalanges and metatarsal bones are big and strong.

The tarsal and metatarsal bones of the foot form a longitudinal arch, which acts as a shock absorber. A transverse arch across the metatarsals helps with weight distribution. The form of the trunk and limbs of *Homo sapiens* is characterized by its adaptation for the fully upright posture, which goes along with this striding bipedal gait.

The selective advantages of bipedalism are immense, in that it frees the hands for the carriage of food, tools and weapons, as well as permitting their development for manipulative purposes.* Although the hominids who came before *Homo sapiens* did make tools, refined work demands hands that are capable of both the power grip – which involves the inner part of the hand, and permits a firm hold to be taken on a branch, a rock, or a case of wine – and the precision grip – which requires that the outer tips of the fingers and thumb be opposed to one another and then brought together, as when holding a small brush to make a cave painting, or coins to get cigarettes out of a vending machine.

The bullet entered my foot between the second and third metatarsals, ricocheting off one and into the other, shattering both. One of the dorsal metatarsal arteries

---

* As in pilfering, backstabbing, management consultancy, etcetera.

was completely severed, as was the second extensor digitorum longus tendon. Yet the entrance wound was remarkably neat. So much so that, when my boot was cut away from my foot and the mess cleaned up, I felt tempted to ask the nurses to check the other foot, just in case a corresponding hole had appeared there too. Foreheads of men have bled where no wounds were, and all that.

But not mine. I was just a sorry fool who had shot himself in the foot.

(highly advanced vegetables)

I'm perhaps not that bad a person in the conventional sense – though I must confess, I did once throw a Scandinavian tourist off the Embankment footbridge. (He was picked up by a passing tourist boat. I knew he'd float; I could tell just by looking at him that he was completely hollow.) But I've always been non-violent towards women, children, animals, and the elderly, and have indulged in many profoundly sentimental acts of charitable giving.

My problem was that I always had everything I wanted, but never wanted the right things. Maybe I didn't know how; maybe I didn't dare. Aphro says that one of the great intellectual errors of the modern world – preached by economists, politicians, and psychologists alike – is the belief that human rationality is concerned only with the means we adopt to achieve our ends. The ends themselves – in other words, the objects of our desires – are no longer subject to rational debate. Any dregs of a life will do, just so long as someone can turn a profit by selling it to you.

Aphro is probably the most rational thing I ever desired. Her responses to the world – her likes and dislikes – are as unlike mine as they possibly could be. She visited me in hospital every day. I told her that I was in love with her and asked her to marry me. She looked a little flustered and then smiled at me and said that we'd see. I think she'll say yes, because there were tears in her eyes, and she had that kind of excited, nowhere look about her that women have when they want to admit someone to their world. I told her that I knew I was a catastrophe, but that with the right kind of encouragement I would evolve into a human being. I told her that I would do everything she wanted me to, because I knew that she would only want what was best.

Max came to see me too. Aphro had been telling me that in so far as two people are friends, each stands in the same relation to the other's good as they do to their own. I told her that it was a good thing that I've never had any friends before now, because, if I had, they'd all be in hospital with gunshot wounds. Then Max put his head round the door. Max was always my friend; that's why he disapproved of me so much. Only the most bitter enemy could have done otherwise.

(Oedipus rex)

She said yes (whatever that means).
I arrived.